THE OWL'S KISS

THE OWL'S KISS

Three Stories by
Mary Q. Steele

Greenwillow Books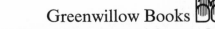
A Division of William Morrow & Company, Inc.
New York

Library of Congress Cataloging
in Publication Data
Steele, Mary Q
The owl's kiss.
Contents: The owl's kiss.—The last great
snake.—Dita's story.
[1. Fantasy] I. Title. PZ7.S81460w
[Fic]   78-1983   ISBN 0-688-80174-9
ISBN 0-688-84174-0 lib. bdg.

TO JUDY MILDRAM
May all her dreams be lovely as herself,
May all her paths be peace.

Contents

THE OWL'S KISS
1

THE LAST GREAT SNAKE
27

DITA'S STORY
81

Author's Note

Although I have used in this book themes and details from folktales and legends of the world, I have used them in my own way and for my own purposes.

The setting is the country of my imagination. The characters are the children of my heart and head.

THE OWL'S KISS

OWLS HAD been trying to kill Herla as far back as she could remember.

One evening when she was very small she had gone with her older cousin Dikina to fetch a melon from her mother's garden. And on the way back to Herla's house an owl had flown over her head, so close that she could feel the stir of air made by its silent wings.

"That owl was trying to kill you," Dikina told her matter-of-factly. "When you were born an owl cried outside your house all night. My mother told me so. I expect you are really an owl's child and they would rather you were dead than be a human child. I expect they do not like to see you eating the stuff from your mother's garden or what your father brings home from the forest. They would rather see you eating grasshoppers and young rabbits."

Herla turned away. She did not want to eat grass-hoppers and mice, as owls did. She did not want to be an owl's child. She wanted to belong to her own mother and father.

She went inside her house and cried a little. Her mother heard her from outside, where she was slicing the melon, and came to comfort her.

"What is it?" her mother asked. "What has made you cry? Was it something Dikina said? He teases too much. You must learn not to pay attention to him."

Herla dried her eyes and felt better. She was not an owl's child.

And she went outside and ate some of the melon. And then she remembered what she had done and she knew why the owl had tried to kill her.

Only that afternoon her mother had gathered a basket of melita fruits for Herla's grandmother. And when her mother was not looking, Herla had eaten three of the fruits herself. She had been very careful, taking only small ones and moving the others so that no one would know that three were missing.

Very often Herla had heard that when old people died, many of them changed into owls. The owl which had tried to kill her must have been one of these. It had spied her when she was stealing the fruit for which her grand-mother had been eagerly waiting. It had tried to kill her because she had done such a wicked thing to her grand-mother, an old person as the owl had once been.

Since that time Herla had watched and listened diligently, and twice she had seen owls watching her from the forest trees, many times she had heard owls calling back and forth to each other that Herla was a wicked girl and that they would pounce on her as they would pounce on a mouse or a vole.

Herla did not go outside at night unless she was with her mother or her father or some other grown person, and she stayed very close to her companion for protection.

"Herla is afraid of the dark," her mother sometimes said, and Herla did not deny it. And she did not tell anyone that she was not afraid of the dark but of the owls that flew and hunted in it.

Sometimes she was afraid to go into the deepest part of the forest because she thought an owl might be abroad in that dimness even though the sun shone brightly beyond the trees.

She particularly feared one big tree, an old tree, warped and full of holes. Owls nested there, her father told her, and had for generations. Herla avoided the tree whenever she could.

And still two years after she had stolen the fruit, an owl tried to kill her again. She had been playing close to her house and time had slipped away and the shadows had grown longer than she had realized. She was going to gather up the stones and twigs with which she had been playing and take them into the house, when a bird, a pretty, gaily colored bird, had lit on the ground in front of her.

The Owl's Kiss · 5

And while Herla watched, an owl had swooped down and gripped the bird in its great talons and carried it away.

Herla left her stones and twigs and hurried into the house. She knew that she had been the owl's intended victim and that the lovely bird had offered itself to save her. She was grateful and wondered why it would do such a thing for a girl who had stolen fruits meant for her own grandmother.

And next day, when she went to gather up her pebbles and twigs, a scarlet feather lay among them. She put it away carefully in a secret place, but one day she took it out and looked at it thoughtfully. A little wind picked it up and whirled it away and she never saw it again.

No more owls tried to kill her, but often at night she woke to hear them calling around the house, making their strange chuckling cries and clacking their stout beaks. She was more frightened than ever and now she would not go out in the dark at all, even with her father or mother.

Then some months after the death of the bright bird, Herla's village was stirred by strange news. A man of the village who was known for his curious ways went to spend a few days at The Rocks. Herla had never been to The Rocks, for the place was far away, but her mother and father had been and they had told her about them, a huge, empty stretch of solid rock with a few cracks and wide chasms, where nothing grew and only a few beetles dared to venture onto the hot, hard surface.

The rock itself was very good for making weapons and tools if one knew the proper way to do it. The man who had betaken himself there was not one of those who had this skill; he went only because it was a remote and unearthly place and he hoped to see there some sight that he might come back and tell the others.

And so he did. In three days he came running and he was filled with wonder and excitement. While he was there, the earth had trembled a bit, as occasionally happens, and the next day there had been new cracks in the rocks. And out of one of the cracks, whether old or new he could not say, a great spout of water had flown up into the air and then subsided. The man had thought it was a one-time thing, an eerie accident of some sort.

But no. It had gone on happening at intervals, a great gush of water leaping high above his head and then falling back.

And strangest of all, the water was hot! Where it touched his skin it scalded and blistered. People crowded around to hear him tell the story over and over, and touch the slight burns on his arm.

"Were you not afraid?" asked one man, and the traveler said he had not been frightened.

"It is a strange thing and I could not think what had caused it," he told him. "But it is not a fearful thing. After I had discovered that the water was hot, I stayed away from it, and that was all."

Some were scornful and said he had burned himself purposely so that he might tell such a wild tale, and he answered that they might go and look for themselves. If they went to The Rocks and walked south for the space of an hour and then east for half again that long, they would see what he had seen. They might have to stand for a while, but sooner or later the water would shoot up into the air and fall hissing back to earth.

And several young men and women the next day made the journey, starting early in the day and returning to the village late at night. Everyone came to hear what they had to say, and what they had to say was that the man's story was true.

Three times they had seen the water go towering up into the sky and then after a little while recede into its crack like a snail drawing back into its shell. A marvelous thing, and to some of them terrifying.

What made this thing and what was its meaning? Perhaps some monster lurked in the crack and spat out hot spittle now and then.

Perhaps some evil being dwelt underground and would try to grab those who came near and boil them.

So it was decided that soon some of the older men would walk to The Rocks and try to discover the source of the fountain of hot water.

Herla had been asleep when all this happened and she was sorry to have missed the excitement and talk when the young men and women had returned.

Yet she was glad not to have had to go out in the

dark. Her mother and her older brother and sister told her about it in the morning, and all the town talked of it.

Three days later five strong men, well armed with spears and knives, set out before sunrise for The Rocks. They did not come back that night, or the next day, and the village was worried and fearful. In the middle of the third day they returned.

They had found the spot and seen the tower of water, they said. They had probed the crack with spears and long sticks and had touched nothing but rock. They had called down to the monster to show itself and there had been no response.

Finally they had dropped many stones into the crack. All that had happened was that the stones flew up into the air the next time the water spouted. And one of the stones had struck a man on the head and knocked him senseless, and they had waited until he had recovered enough to make the long walk back to the village.

They had agreed that whatever this thing was it was harmless. Like the first man's burns, the injury from the stone had been an accident, because they had not expected it.

Let the spout of water continue and let those who wished to see go, as long as they took care. It was no more to be explained than snow or thunder and could hurt only those who allowed it to hurt by not keeping the proper distance.

Many in the village were eager to see this marvelous

new sight. Many went and returned with strange stories of how high the water sprang into the air and how long it had continued and how many times it had done this during the time they were there.

Herla's father went, with his brother and another man. They had had to leave an hour before daybreak and it was long past dark when they returned. But Herla's father had found the long walk pleasant and the sight of the tower of water thrilling. And so a few days later he went again and took Herla's older brother and sister with him.

And then he went a third time and Herla's mother grew angry and reminded him that his family needed meat. So he hunted and came home with food.

And in a few days Herla's mother went with some others to see the spouting water. She left before Herla was awake and was gone all day and late into the night. Herla could not sleep because her mother was away and she was not accustomed to such an unusual circumstance. She lay listening for her mother's footsteps and she heard the owls talking among themselves and she was afraid.

Soon almost everyone in the village had seen this curious thing at least once. Herla's mother said she would go again and take Herla. But Herla did not wish to go. The way to The Rocks led by the old tree where the owls made their home. Going and coming one had to walk a long time in the dark.

"I would get tired, I think," she told her mother and her mother laughed.

"You walk farther than that running about the house and garden all day," she said.

Still she did not press Herla to go.

Dikina and his mother and father came to Herla's house one day and said they planned to journey to the spouting water on the following morning.

"Herla can come too," said Dikina's mother. "We would like her company."

And Herla said, "I promised my grandmother I would help her in her garden tomorrow."

"Grandmother will wait for you to come another day," said Dikina's mother.

But Herla shook her head, although it was not true that she had made such a promise.

"Tomorrow will be fair," she said. "Another time it might rain."

So in the morning Herla went to her grandmother's house and worked in the garden. Her grandmother was old and her husband was dead and she was glad of Herla's help.

And anyway they were very fond of one another. Herla did not know how she could have stolen the melita fruits from her grandmother, who loved her best of all her grandchildren and told her stories and made funny small toys out of twigs and nuts and fruit pits for her.

"I was very young and perhaps I did not know better," Herla told herself.

But she had known better and she had rearranged the fruits in the basket so that no one would be able to tell that some of them were gone. The melita fruits were hard to find in the forest and some years there were none to be found at all. They were her grandmother's favorite.

They had been Herla's favorite too until she stole those three. After that, melita fruits had never tasted quite so good again, reminding her as they did how she had stolen. So that day she worked very hard, trying to make up for this bad thing, and at the end of the day she was tired.

Her grandmother said, "I am proud of you, little granddaughter. You have worked almost as hard as a grown woman. Now my garden is bound to thrive and produce much."

And Herla was glad. She hoped the owls heard those words.

Dikina returned from his journey in high spirits. He told everyone about the water as though he were the only one to have seen it. Especially he told Herla, over and over.

"The water comes out of the rock, all at once, and grows up like a great tree and spreads out at the top a little. And then from so high, high, it turns down upon itself and crashes back to the rock. It does this every little while. And my father went with me close enough so that one drop fell upon my hand and it was boiling hot."

He held out his hand for Herla to see, but she saw only his young, tough palm.

"And you, Herla, have never even been to The Rocks, much less seen the great tree of water."

He looked at her sadly. She knew he was not sad. He was pleased to have something to tease her about.

"I do not care," Herla replied. "Soon I will be bigger and then I will go."

"The water may be gone by then," Dikina told her. "My father says it cannot continue forever. Whatever is making the water fly up into the air will grow tired and soon it will sleep or die."

Herla hoped that this was not true. With all her heart she longed to see The Rocks and the mysterious spouting water and feel a hot drop on her own hand. With all her heart she wished she had not stolen the fruit and made the owls angry with her so that they were determined to kill her.

But she could never walk past the owls' tree in the darkness, as one must do, not once but twice, to make the journey.

Dikina told her again of the marvelous sight and how he planned to go a second time before it ceased. His father had promised him he might.

"Now I will go and tell Grandmother," said Dikina. "She too has not seen the water. She will like hearing about how I went to see it."

And this was so. Grandmother had not walked to The Rocks since the water had sprung from its hiding place. She was a strong walker and had made that journey many times, and much longer ones. Still she had not gone to see the strange leaping water and it made Herla feel a little better that there was one other person in the town who had not been, especially since that other person was her grandmother.

And then one day not long after, Grandmother came to Herla's house and said she planned to go to The Rocks.

"Will you go alone?" asked Herla's mother.

"Yes, unless Herla would like to come with me," Grandmother answered.

"Herla says it is too far a walk for her," said Herla's mother.

"To go and come in one day might tire such small legs," said Grandmother. "But I shall not do that. It might tire my old legs too. I will leave one morning after sunrise and see the spouting water and come back before evening next day. That will make the walking easier and we will not have to hurry."

Herla rejoiced. She would not have to pass the owls' tree in the dark. Her grandmother would be with her at all times and they would not be out after dark.

"I will go with Grandmother," she told her mother. "I would like to see The Rocks and the strange tree of water."

Grandmother smiled. "Very well," she said. "We will leave the day after tomorrow."

And Herla was happy.

The sun was just coming up and the day was cool when Herla and her grandmother set out. Grandmother carried a basket full of things to eat. They went into the forest and walked slowly and talked as they went.

Grandmother took Herla a little way from the trail, along a smaller, almost hidden path, to a secret place where flowers grew lovelier than any Herla had ever seen before.

"You must not tell," Grandmother said. "I've never told. My grandmother showed me this secret place when I was your age and told me I might someday show it to my granddaughter. And so I have. But you too must keep the secret and then someday perhaps you can show it to your granddaughter."

They went back to the broad trail and Grandmother pointed out to Herla places where strange or exciting or pleasant things had happened when she was a girl. A place where a man had found a queer dead beast like no beast ever seen before or since. A place where a woman had been killed by stones falling from the sky. And another place where Grandmother, when she was scarcely older than Herla was now, had seen a flock of huge scarlet birds stalking through the trees. Herla could almost see them herself, long-legged and glowing like coals among the dark trunks.

They passed by the owls' tree and Herla walked close beside her grandmother and nothing happened. Only Grandmother said, as Herla's father had said, that owls had nested in the holes of the tree for many years, since long before Grandmother was born.

It was nearly noon and Herla was hungry and growing a little tired.

Grandmother said, "We will stop here and have something to eat and rest a little while. It is not far now to The Rocks."

They found a comfortable place to sit and ate some of the good things from Grandmother's basket. And then they stayed a little while, resting and listening to the forest sounds.

Herla was eager to go on, longing to see The Rocks and the spire of water shooting from that flat surface. But she waited patiently. Grandmother would know best when they were ready to continue.

And by and by Grandmother rose and covered the basket with a cloth once more and they began to walk again. Herla's heart raced with excitement. She was farther from home than she had ever been before in her lifetime and the strangest sights of her lifetime lay just ahead.

And then they were there.

They came out of the forest and there before Herla's astonished eyes spread the miles and miles and miles of bare gray rock, rolling away toward the edge of the world. Herla was a little disappointed, for it seemed to her bleak and ugly, although no one had told her it would be beautiful, only different from the green world of forests and fields which she had always known.

Still there was the spout of water yet to see and they followed the directions everyone had given them, many times over, and came to the proper place and stood waiting. They knew it was the proper place, for here many people had built small fires and someone had dropped a clay pot and the shards lay scattered all about.

For a little while Grandmother and Herla saw or heard nothing that would indicate where the water would come from. And then suddenly from one of the nearby cracks there came a strange gurgling sound. Grandmother drew Herla back, for they were too close, and the water shot up out of the crevice and into the sky and spread a little at the top and came hurtling down upon itself in a great splash of rainbowed steam and was gone.

Three times more during the hours they waited there it happened, and each time it seemed to Herla more wonderful and exciting than before. What could make such a thing happen, the tall column of water climbing up and up into the clear air and then falling back, hissing and spitting and disappearing into the crack or lying in small pools on the stone for a moment before it vanished in little mists of steam?

Grandmother laughed aloud to see and even Herla smiled, although she was more than a little awed. But she was happy to have come to The Rocks while this eerie thing still went on and when it had not died as her uncle had predicted that it would. And she was happy to have come with her grandmother, who was seeing it for the first time too.

At last Grandmother said they must go and they started back the way they had come. Once Herla turned to watch for the spouting water one last time and when she saw the sky deepening in the east she knew that darkness would soon come.

"Grandmother, where shall we sleep?" she asked.

"In a pleasant, mossy place I know, just inside the forest's edge," answered Grandmother.

Herla stopped. She had not greatly thought until then of where they would spend the night. She had not supposed they would lie in the open. She had imagined Grandmother would know of a shelter of some sort, a hut of wood or a tent of skins.

"Come along," said Grandmother. "We should hurry a little."

Herla came after her. She hurried. Their shadows stretched far behind them across the bare rock and it began to seem to Herla a terrible place, not only ugly but full of horror.

Oh, she should not have come. She should have stayed with her mother and not let it bother her that she of all the village had not seen the leaping water.

And soon it would be night and owls would surely find her and kill her. Her grandmother would be sleeping and owls would fly silently down and seize Herla in their strong, cruel talons and peck out her eyes and pull her to pieces. She clung to her grandmother's hand and they walked on.

It was dim twilight when they reached the forest's edge. Grandmother sat down and uncovered her basket and gave Herla something to eat. She had brought all the things Herla liked best.

But Herla could not eat. She could not chew or swallow. She sat with her supper in her hands and stared into the thickening shadows.

"What is it, Herla?" asked her grandmother. "Are you not hungry?"

And Herla took one bite and then another, but the rest of the food she pushed down among the grasses when her grandmother was not looking.

"Now we will sleep," said Grandmother. "I will sleep there on that stretch of moss and you shall sleep here, on this smaller bit."

"Can I not sleep beside you, Grandmother?" Herla whispered.

"I think we would disturb each other," answered Grandmother. "I will be quite close by. Are you afraid of the dark, Herla?"

"A little," said Herla.

"There is nothing to be afraid of," Grandmother told her. "There is nothing in our forest to harm anyone. By day you often go into the forest alone. And now most creatures are sleeping, as you and I should be."

She went over and lay down on her bed of moss, and Herla lay down too. But she did not sleep. Starlight faintly lit the forest and she strained to see into the trees. Once she thought she heard an owl call, but she was not certain. And anyway tonight the owls need not call to one another, talking of Herla. Tonight they would know where she lay and they could see her, though she, having eyes made for daylight, could not see them.

She was so frightened that she might have died of fear, except that then she heard her grandmother breathing regularly and evenly and knew the old woman was asleep. Stealthily Herla crawled toward her and lay down as near to her as she could without truly touching.

Would the owls dare come for her now, so close to her grandmother, who was still strong and might be able to protect Herla? Herla did not know.

She lay awake a long time, watching and listening. And then suddenly she heard, quite close, an owl's long, low chuckling cry.

Herla cried out. She could not help it. Her terror was too great, she could not keep it prisoned inside her any longer.

Grandmother sat up, startled out of sleep.

"Herla, what is it? Where are you?" she cried.

Herla began to weep.

"Oh, I am here, Grandmother," she sobbed. "And owls are coming to kill me!"

Grandmother put her arms around the little girl and held her until she ceased to cry.

"Why would owls want to kill you?" she asked gently.

Herla put her hands over her face. She could not tell the truth.

"Because I am really an owl's child and they do not like to see me living with human beings," she said. "They would rather I were dead than see me eating human food and wearing human clothes, not feathers."

Grandmother laughed a little.

"What gave you such a notion?" she asked. "You are your mother's and your father's child. Owls have children of their own. And they could never have a child who was afraid of the dark."

Herla began to cry again.

"Oh, Grandmother, that is what Dikina told me," she said. "But it is not true. Owls are trying to kill me because I stole from you and they saw it. Owls are old people come back to earth after death, and they did not like it that I stole from my grandmother. And so they have twice tried to kill me already, and I have not gone out in the dark because of that. And now they have seen me here and perhaps even you cannot save me."

"When did owls try to kill you?" asked Grandmother, and Herla told. She told how Dikina had said she was an owl's child and that was the reason for the first owl's attack.

"But oh, it was not, Grandmother," said Herla sorrowfully. "It was because when my mother gathered melita fruits for you that day, I stole three from the basket. And I moved the fruits so that no one would know that three were missing."

"Why did you not ask your mother for some of them?" Grandmother questioned her.

And Herla did not answer though she knew why. If she had asked, her mother would have given her some. But her mother had been proud of being able to take so many fine melita fruits to Grandmother. If her mother had shared them with Herla, she would not have felt so pleased. So Herla had stolen.

"It is always wrong to steal," Grandmother told her. "But it is especially bad to steal from old ones for they often have less of good things and more troubles than young people. Still I do not believe owls are trying to kill you. Not for three melita fruits."

She sat for a moment holding Herla to her and the owl called again, its strange, hollow, purring cry.

Then Grandmother went on, "I will tell you a secret. You have said that when old people die they sometimes come back to earth as owls. It is true, and I am one of those who may return in owl form. And since I am so old and close to death, by which I do not mean that I am ill or dying but that I am of an age when death cannot be far from me, for this reason I can speak to owls.

"I will speak to them now and ask if they intend you harm. And if they do, I will ask them to forgive such a small theft so long ago. And they will, for my sake."

She released Herla and stood up. And then she uttered the owls' calls, over and over. After a few minutes many owls came on noiseless wings and settled in the trees about them and even on the ground.

Herla could see their round eyes shining faintly and hear their beaks clack softly and sternly. She was afraid.

They spoke to Grandmother in all their ghostly voices, in low whistles and hoots and long, sad, tremulous murmurs and sudden harsh, almost croaking sounds. And she answered them in kind. They talked for many minutes.

And then the largest of the owls flew down from a tree and lit beside Grandmother in the pale starlight, and Grandmother said to Herla, "Owls do not wish to harm you. They remember those times you have spoken about and both things happened by accident and chance. They wish to be your friends. And this one is here to give you the owl's kiss, to show that they are your friends and never wish to hurt you. Come, go to him and stoop down and you will see."

Herla did not wish the owl's kiss. She did not wish to go near the big owl. But she was accustomed to obeying her grandmother and so she did as she was bade.

She took a few slow steps toward the owl and knelt down. The owl came forward and she looked into his round, gleaming eyes and into their dark depths, mysterious and full of night. For a long time she gazed, and then the owl put his round, tufted head against her cheek and gently, gently nibbled along it with his stout, hooked beak. His soft feathers pressed against her cheek and she could smell a faint, strange scent of mouse and rotted wood and shadows.

Then the owl reached up and pulled from her head, quickly and easily so that she scarcely felt it, one of her long, dark hairs. He flew away then and after a minute Herla stood up. All the owls spoke for a little and their voices seemed to Herla kind and loving.

"There," said Grandmother, "he has taken one of the

hairs of your head and it will make a bond of friendship between them and you and you will not be afraid again."

"No," said Herla and she was not afraid. "Owls are my friends."

"And you too when you are old may understand their talk," said Grandmother. "And you may come back to earth in owl form if you so wish. But that is a great time from here."

And so the owls flew away and Herla and her grandmother went to sleep on their beds of moss.

In the morning Herla imagined that it had all been a dream, but Grandmother said, "Remember always what has happened here and how you had the owl's kiss."

"I will always remember," Herla promised. She was glad that it had not been a dream, that it had all truly happened and she need no longer be afraid of owls or be frightened of going out in the dark.

But still she was a little troubled and at last she said, "Grandmother, I have never stolen from anyone since that time I took the melita fruits. And I will never steal from anyone again. But oh, Grandmother, if I had not done that bad thing, I would not be the owls' friend and have the owl's kiss."

Grandmother smiled a little. "And now you know what owls know and what I know," she said. "Sometimes out of a wicked thing a good thing can come. In our lives we all do many bad things and we suffer for them and so some good must come of them on occasion. Owls are wise and they know that."

And since this was what owls and Grandmother knew, it must be true, Herla thought, and she felt better.

On the way home they passed the owls' tree. Herla looked up and was not afraid. She thought she heard a rustle of feathers, as though the owls knew that she and Grandmother were going by and sent them a greeting.

When they walked back into the village, Dikina came to meet them.

"Did you walk the long way to The Rocks?" he asked.

"Yes," answered Herla. "And we saw the spouting water. We saw it many times."

"I expect I saw it spout more often," said Dikina. "I expect it spouted higher when we were there."

Herla didn't care what Dikina said.

"I expect I will go back some day and spend the night, the way you did," he went on. "I will spend two days maybe, and two nights, and watch the spouting water for many hours."

And Herla did not care.

The days went by and Herla's mother said, "Herla is not afraid of the dark any more," and Herla smiled. She was not afraid. Even when owls came close to the house and called back and forth, she was not afraid.

She went into the deepest, dimmest parts of the forest and was no longer frightened. She went in search of melita fruits, for she was growing tall now and learning to do such things for her mother. And once on such an errand, she heard an owl call even though it was day, and she followed its voice and came upon a melita tree covered with fruit, more than she had known could be. And she brought her basket home filled to the edges and her mother and father praised her, but Herla knew it was the owl's doing.

And the strange fountain of water continued and Herla sometimes went to see it, with Dikina and others.

And when in the dark they passed the owls' tree, she felt the bond of friendship between herself and the birds of night, and she was glad.

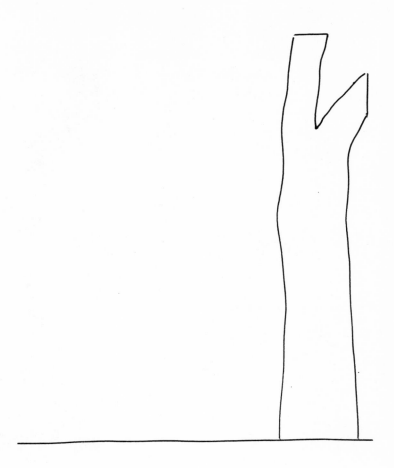

THE LAST GREAT
SNAKE

BALA WAS sitting by his fireside, carefully polishing his spearhead, when Gatani appeared in the circle of light. Bala stared at him and said nothing.

"I have come for my magic stone," said Gatani at last.

"Have you indeed?" responded Bala. He rubbed sand furiously along the edge of his spearhead.

Gatani was silent. He seemed to be waiting. Bala did not look at him. When Gatani spoke again, his voice was cold with anger. "You have stolen my magic stone. Everyone knows you have stolen it. And now I have come for it."

Bala continued to polish the spear with much energy. When he was done with one side, he turned it over.

"I have not stolen your stone," he answered evenly. "What everyone knows and what is true are not always the same thing. I know nothing of your stone. I have not seen it."

Gatani clenched his fists. His breath hissed between his lips. "The stone was in my house," he whispered. "Now it is gone. Three people saw you leave my house. Three people. Only you could have taken my magic stone."

His eyes blazed above the fire. Then he turned and walked away into the darkness.

Bala went on with his polishing.

In the morning he went to the market, for he had some skins to trade. Anyway he always went to the market on those mornings when he did not hunt. It was a good time to see his friends and hear whatever news there was to hear. He sat down in his usual place, but no one came to ask about his pelts, though Bala and his wife had prepared them carefully.

Bala's wife wished to trade for seeds for her garden and the stuff with which to make a new fish net and perhaps a small metal ornament for her little daughter's neck.

The people in the market did not speak to Bala. Many even turned their heads and would not look at him. He sat a long time and no one came to trade with him.

Then he knew in fact that his honor was gone and everyone truly believed he had stolen Gatani's magic stone.

He gathered up his skins and carried them back to his home and laid them on a shelf. He took two or three tubers and some bread and his spear and his knife and walked away.

He did not speak to anyone and there were few to see him go, for those who were not hunting or gardening were at the market.

Bala did not say good-bye to his wife and his son and daughter. His wife would be working with her plants and her children would be with her. She need not look again upon her husband, a man without honor.

Her father and brothers would help her and soon people would forget. Perhaps someday another man would marry her. It seemed unlikely. Another man would not want the care of Bala's children, the son and daughter of the one who had stolen Gatani's magic stone.

Bala did not walk on the trail, for he did not want to meet anyone. He walked well away from the marked path, among the trees. And he went quietly, so that no one would hear him, so that he might hear others coming toward him in time to shelter himself behind a tree.

He had no wish to look into the face of anyone who supposed that Bala would do such a thing, would steal anything at all, much less Gatani's magic stone. The stone was not really Gatani's. It had come to him from his grandfather, who had been dead for many years.

Who would steal from an old dead man?

Bala walked softly and thought about the magic stone, which had lain in a carved box in Gatani's house ever since the old man died. No one but Gatani and a few of the honored old men of the village had seen it. It was said to be a clear and colorless stone and in its depth one could see true things, what had been and what was to come.

Gatani fed it every week with the blood of certain animals, mixed with fresh spring water. Sometimes he dared to look into its depths and see the truth, what had been and what was to come. He did not do it often. It was a dangerous thing to do, for the truth might crack a heart or make a brain go numb forever.

Bala saw a hare among the bushes and killed it with his spear to eat for supper. He was a good hunter. His family had never lacked for meat or hides. He had no reason to steal, not even a magic stone.

He picked up the hare and looked at it. Yet he had indeed gone into Gatani's house. Gatani's wife had no sense. She had left her fish lying by the door and gone away. Bala had watched and waited for her to come back, and when a crow flew down to eat the catch, Bali had frightened it off and himself taken the fish inside the house and laid them on the hearth.

Three people were passing when he came out and no one thought it strange.

Only the next day, when Gatani opened the carved box to feed the stone and discovered that it was missing, only then had three people come forward and told how Bala had been alone in Gatani's house. Had gone inside when Gatani was away hunting and his wife gone to fetch water to boil her fish.

Bala was angry with these people and yet he knew they had done what they thought was right. To steal was a dreadful thing. And to steal a magic stone was more dreadful still.

A magic stone, a clear and flashing crystal from the head of the giant snake Conokili, a stone which had once caused rain to fall when the forests were almost parched to powder and the gardens yielding nothing.

Bala could remember that terrible year himself, though he had been very young at the time. The stone's rightful owner, Gatani's grandfather, had done that terrifying thing, had dared to go to the stone and ask that it make the rain fall and the thunder roll. But then Gatani's grandfather had been a man of huge courage anyway, for he had killed the giant snake Conokili and taken the stone from its head in the first place.

Bala walked on, deeper and deeper into the forest. When night fell he made a small fire and cooked his supper. And when he had polished his spear carefully, he lay down and went to sleep and over his head passed the silent stars and a dark moon.

But in his house in the village his wife lay awake and heard the cry of owls, for she did not believe that Bala was a man who had stolen a magic crystal.

Nevertheless, she knew that in leaving he had done the only thing he could do, and she spent that night in sorrow for him and for herself and for their children. In the early morning she rose and went a little way into the forest and buried the skins he had left on the shelf.

But she did not forget the spot where they lay, and it was a little as if she had buried Bala there. And sometimes she would come and stand awhile near the place and sometimes she brought her son and daughter with her.

In four days her father came to take them away to live with him in his house. But she would not go.

"I will stay here," she told him.

Her father was a kind man and he saw that she wished to stay in her own house with her memories and her hope that Bala would someday return there. Yet he was a proud man and knew that if she went on living there alone, everyone in the village would mark it. They would remember Bala and what he had done and that she had been wife to a man who had lost his honor.

So her father went away in some anger, but every week he brought her meat from his hunting and asked if she needed anything.

And time went by.

Day after day Bala walked deeper into the forest, farther and farther away from his home. Now he walked upon a trail, for he no longer feared meeting someone who might recognize him. He was in a place he did not know, a long way from any hunting ground he had ever traveled over.

And then one day he met a party of hunters. They were strangers to him, every one, yet he had some notion of where they came from. He had seen before the kind of weapons they carried and he knew what villagers used them.

They halted when they saw him, and he knew they too must have identified the place he came from, by his spear and his clothes, and must be wondering what he was doing here, alone, and far from home.

The men greeted him politely. They wished him well and all his family and friends, and he returned the greeting.

Then one of them asked, "Have you seen a great and strange beast as you journeyed?"

Bala shook his head. "No," answered Bala. "Only hare and small deer and such. And not many of them."

"Have you seen the tracks or any other sign of such a beast?" asked another.

"I have seen nothing unusual," Bala replied. He wanted to know what kind of beast they were hunting and why, but he did not ask. In time they would tell him, and in time they did.

"A great and strange beast has attacked our village," they explained. "It has trampled our gardens and made a wallow in our stream and knocked down a tall tree. It has come twice now and our town is afraid. So we have gone hunting it, to kill it and keep it from coming back to do such damage again."

"What does it look like?" asked Bala and they shrugged their shoulders.

The Last Great Snake · 35

"We do not know," they told him. "It comes at night. We are afraid and stay in our houses and hope it does not trample us."

"It is tall and has an eye that blazes in the dark," put in one who must have been brave enough to peek out of his door.

But the rest gave him scornful looks to show that they did not believe him and did not think he had been so brave.

"We do not know," repeated the first man who had spoken. "We only judge it to be large and fierce, for it knocked down a tall tree."

"I have seen no sign of a large beast," Bala told them again and he went his way.

He left them reluctantly for they were the only company of any kind he had had since leaving his house. He would have hunted with them for a while, but they traveled toward his village and he must travel the other way. And when he came to a point where the trail divided, he took the road which led away from their town.

On the next day he met again a hunting party, and they were from some very distant place and were after certain birds, the feathers of which were needed for a ceremonial costume for their priest. They scarcely spoke, for their mission was a sacred one and they were not allowed to spend time in idle talk. Their faces were solemn and the few words they said to him were hushed and quiet.

36 ·

For a week Bala met no one else and walked in the green forest and heard the voices of birds and scurry of small creatures in the underbrush and the sounds of water rushing in streams. It was hot and oppressive and then one night there was a huge storm, heavy rains, and lightning flashing and flashing, and thunder like the growls and grumbles of mountains stirred by anger.

Bala was frightened and crouched under a bush and let the water pour over him. In the glitter of the lightning he saw the trees bend and sway, and once he heard the sound of some giant of the forest crashing and falling, and once the mournful, fearful howl of a wolf.

The storm went away, but the rain went on and on, and Bala could not hunt or cook. He ate roots and berries and walked on.

When at last the rain stopped, he had reached the banks of a river. Here there must have been a ford at other times, but now there was only a furious sea full of sticks and branches and even whole trees rushing past.

The bodies of animals whirled by on the current and he tried to reach one, thinking he might find a way to cook it, for he was painfully hungry. He waded out into the stream as far as he dared and with a stick tried to entangle the antlers of a deer and haul it to the shore. He slipped and nearly went in, so he did not try again.

He sat and waited for the stream to subside and thought about his wife and children and wondered if the storm had come upon them and if they were safe and well.

He did not think about them often, for he had made up his mind not to. He was a man without honor and he had no right to long for his home and his family. Yet now he could not seem to avoid thinking about them, and at last, made restless by his memories and fears, he got up and plunged into the river.

The torrent was not so strong and violent as it had been and he believed he could swim across. He had not eaten properly for a long time and his arms and legs might not have all their powers, still he thought he would try.

The current pulled and pushed at him and dragged at him with long muscular tentacles. He struggled to make some progress and was drawn under and shoved this way and that and grew more and more tired trying to keep his head above the surface. He gave up and drifted with the river, but he did not drown.

Instead the water seized him and bore him roughly downstream and cast him roughly upon the opposite bank where the river made a sudden bend.

He lay there gasping and panting and grateful that he had not drowned. It surprised him that a man without honor should be grateful to find himself still alive.

Bala journeyed on. There was more game to be had now, and he ate well and felt stronger. Every night he made his fire and cooked his meals and polished his spear. Sometimes he whetted his knife.

The country through which he passed was not like his own country. The forest was thinner, the trees and undergrowth more scattered, and the land flatter. There was still a trail to follow, and people must live nearby, but Bala saw none of them and did not come upon a town or even a house. A hunting trail perhaps.

And then one day he did see something coming toward him along the path. Not a hunter, but a strange shimmering yellow shape, a vague, pale golden outline. Bala was frightened and stopped, but he stayed in the trail and the thing came toward him.

It was almost upon him before he realized what it was. A great river of yellow butterflies was coming toward him, a flowing stream of thousands upon thousands of fluttering wings the color of spring sunlight.

They came closer and closer and he stood still with fast-beating heart, for he did not know what such a crowd of living creatures might do to him. They danced up and down in the air like blown leaves, but when they came up to him, they parted like a stream of water and flowed on either side of him and all their wings whispered past his ears. He did not move, and now and then some of them paused and lit upon his shoulders and his thighs and on the wooden handle of his spear and on his head. Their touch was no more than the touch of air stirred by a small warm wind.

He was frightened still for there seemed no end to their numbers. They went by and went by and went by, until he was dazzled and dizzied. He had never seen or heard of such a thing before and he suspected it was a magic. So many wings, so many butterflies, more than he had known existed in all the world, so thick on either side of him he could scarcely glimpse the trees beside the trail. A magician must have created them—perhaps an evil magician.

And then suddenly they were gone. A last little drift floated past him and then a straggle of two or three and then nothing at all.

Bala did not turn his head to look after them. He was still frightened at so amazing a happening and he did not wish to see more of them.

Yet after a while he thought perhaps it had been a sign, a portent that his journey would soon end.

And the very next day he emerged from the forest and found himself in a long valley of green grasses. In the distance he could see strange formations of dull white rocks. He walked toward the nearest of them and saw with shock that they were not rocks at all. In the grass lay bones, enormous bones, the bones of some animal far bigger than any creature Bala had ever seen. Rib bones taller than himself and teeth bigger than his fist and long, long tusks.

Once again he was filled with fear and thought to leave this valley. But it was a pleasant green place, the grass was soft and deep, rabbits and birds were there in plenty. So he stayed.

And after a while he knew that he had been meant to find this place and live there. For a man without honor is like a bone stripped of its flesh and this should be his home from now on. He would be a bone and live among bones.

There were a few small springs here and there. Rushes grew around them and insects hovered over them. Bala chose the biggest and clearest of these springs and made his fire nearby.

Although it was warm and he had no trouble finding food, he knew that winter would come and with it cold weather and rain or snow. He built a house, using the awesome bones. He made a hut by standing some of the rib bones up and leaning them against each other in a sort of circle. And then he wound grasses and reeds in and out of the bones and plastered the whole thing over with mud and more grass, and he fashioned a door of skins.

He found a rock for the hearth in the middle of the house and there was a hole in the center of the roof, where the rib bones did not quite meet, and out of this hole the smoke from his hearth could drift up into the open sky.

When it was done, it was a good house, and he went inside and kindled a small fire and sat by it and polished his spear and whetted his knife.

But when it came time to sleep, he went outside and lay on the ground, for he did not yet feel easy in his house of bones. Only when the weather grew so cold that he could not sleep comfortably did he begin to spend his nights indoors.

And he waited for whatever would happen next.

When the first snow fell, he rose from his bed and went out his skin door into the world which had changed, since he first came here, from green to brown to white. The huge bones looked lusterless and weatherbeaten and ancient, looming up in the snow. They looked almost tan against the new whiteness.

He wondered what dreadful animals had come here to die and leave their skeletons for him to find. He wondered if anyone else knew of this valley and if other people ever came here.

Almost at once a man appeared, a man older than himself, with a tired, thin face and stringy arms. A hunter with a spear. But the spear was not polished and sharp-edged and shining, like Bala's. It was dull and useless-looking.

The two stood staring at each other, and at last the older man spoke.

"I have come here searching for game," he said. "I see you have come here to live." He nodded at Bala's hut.

Bala was polite. "I did not mean to intrude on land belonging to others," he replied. "I have seen no one except you since I have been here. I will leave if this is a place where I should not have made my dwelling."

The man smiled a little. "This place belongs to no one but the bones of the great creatures which once lived and died here. Many believe that it belongs to their ghosts or to evil witches or bad spirits. I do not know of anyone who wants to live here except yourself. I come here to hunt. I am no longer young and my eyes trouble me. To find meat and skins for my family grows harder and harder. Here there are rabbits at least. And sometimes deer and other things. When I come home empty-handed for many days, then I travel to this place and hunt where few others hunt. I usually kill something."

"Have you no sons to hunt for you?" asked Bala.

The man shook his head. "My wife and my two sons died many years ago, in a plague," he answered. "And then when I was too old, foolishly I married again and my new wife and I have a young daughter, but no sons. My wife is a good and patient woman, she works hard in the garden, she fishes and sometimes she traps birds. But we are in need of skins. And other things."

He hesitated and then went on sadly, "Our village is small. And somehow we do not seem to have many children. Not enough to take care of all of us who are growing old. We try to help each other out. I do what I can."

Bala felt sorry for the other man. And yet he had not lost his honor. He was still part of his village.

But Bala said nothing of his own troubles and why he was here. It was too terrible a thing to say aloud. Not yet.

"We will hunt together, you and I," he said. "I know

where we can find deer. I do not need so much meat. I will share whatever we find and you may have the skin. I am not in need of skins."

The other man bowed his head.

"You are kind," he replied. "But I have seen the deer's tracks in the snow. I will hunt alone today. If I have no luck, tomorrow perhaps I can go with you."

Bala saw how it was. This man wanted to hunt for his family by himself. He did not want the company of a stranger, one who lived in this queer valley full of bones and ghosts. He perhaps could sense that Bala was a man who had lost his honor.

The man walked away. The sun came out and most of the snow melted. Bala busied himself at his few tasks. He killed a hare.

In the evening the other man returned, but he had no deer with him. "I lost their tracks when the snow melted," he said. "I searched a long time and I did not find them again."

"Share my supper," said Bala. "It is too much for one and I have no trouble getting hares and rabbits. They are all about."

"Thank you," said the other man.

He came in Bala's house and laid his spear to one side and sat by the hearth. They ate in silence and then once again Bala polished and sharpened his spear. To make talk, he told the man how he had met the villagers whose town had been threatened by a great beast.

"Do you suppose it might be such a beast as died here?" Bala asked.

The man considered. "Perhaps," he answered. "I have never heard of one being seen alive. But that is no reason to believe they do not exist. The world is full of wonders no one has ever seen. There are some who say the great snake Ulukini lives in the hills to the north of this valley still. One last giant snake with a magic crystal in its head."

Bala's heart beat fast. Did this man know who he was and that everyone supposed him to be the thief of Gatani's magic stone? But his hands went on polishing and polishing, smoothly and quickly, and did not falter.

"As you say, there are many strange things in the world," he said at last.

He laid down his spear and picked up the other man's. As though in absent-mindedness he polished it too, until it glistened and the edges were sharp and keen. Then he lay down and went to sleep.

The next morning there was more snow. The two hunted together and before noon each had killed a small deer.

"I have meat and skins in plenty," Bala told the other man. "You may take my deer to your family. I would not want to waste so much, and so much would waste if I were to keep it."

Again the man bent his head and did not look at Bala. "I am grateful," he responded. "You are a very kind man."

The Last Great Snake · 45

He said nothing more but kept his eyes on the ground so that Bala might not read there the question he did not speak: Why are you living alone in this strange place of long-dead beasts and ghosts?

He went away, carrying the two deer, and Bala watched him go.

And time went by.

The winter was not very cold or very long, and soon the grass grew up and turned green among the bones and bright flowers blossomed here and there. Bala busied himself as best he could. He grew used to his surroundings and it no longer seemed so curious and uncanny to live in a house made of enormous ribs or to stumble over a vast tusk half-buried in the earth.

Yet it was lonely still and grew no less lonely. And Bala had every day to make his mind turn away from thoughts of his wife and children, of his home and his friends in the market place.

He missed too the tasseled trees of spring and the returning birds, for in this valley there were few trees and only small ones. And the birds were not the soaring singing birds of the forest but mostly ground birds with quiet sad voices and dim colors.

Some days he walked the long distance to the hills toward the north to stand among the big trees and watch their new leaves unfolding and to see the birds, scarlet and blue and green, which flew among the branches. And he would look up and think about the giant snake which lived in the peaks of the mountains, with a magic stone like Gatani's in its head.

And time went by.

And then one morning he woke and stood up and looked about him. Now that the weather was warm he once again slept in the open, unless it rained. Two figures were coming toward him across the green grasses of the valley. He waited, and when they came closer, he saw that it was an old woman and a boy, a boy about fourteen years old.

They did not come to him but stopped some way off. They saw him, he was quite sure, and he wondered why they did not walk closer to look at him and perhaps speak to him, but they did not.

They made a sort of camp and for two days they lived there without appearing to pay him any attention. He was tempted to go to them, to offer them some of the hares and rabbits and birds he killed for food. He did not go. He was a man without honor and must wait for others to come to him.

At last the old woman approached his house one afternoon. She did not speak. She walked about his house several times, inspecting it carefully. She even lifted the skin door and peered inside.

Then she went away.

During the next few days she and the boy worked together and made themselves a similar hut of rib bones and mud and grass. It was not so good a house as Bala's and again he bethought himself to go to offer help. Not until he saw the old woman struggling to carry in a hearthstone did he travel the distance to their home and take the stone from her and carry it inside and place it where it should go and settle it into the earth.

They did not speak, not even when he went outside and rearranged some of the grasses and mud and reeds in some places to make the walls more weather-resistant. When he was done, he stepped back and looked it over, and then the old woman addressed him.

"I give you thanks," she said. "Your help was needed. I am old and my grandson is young and we neither of us have the strength for doing such tasks properly."

"Why did you not ask for my help?" asked Bala. "I am a grown man and strong and have little to do with my time. I would have liked helping you make your house."

The old woman fell silent once again. She gazed off into the west, in the direction from which they had come. Her hair was long and tangled and her clothes were worn and tattered and hung in ragged streamers about her knees.

Finally she said, "When we came here, I thought we should be alone. I did not think that someone else would be living here. It is best that my grandson and I have nothing to do with other people. I knew of no other place to go, so we stayed here. But I thought it wisest to act as if we were alone here. To act as if you were some kind of harmless beast living nearby and to treat you thus. When we have been here longer, perhaps I will think of some way we can be neighbors, even friends. But not yet."

"My name is Bala," said Bala. "I can hunt for you. I am a good hunter. I can supply meat and skins for you, at least."

"My grandson is a good hunter too," replied the old woman. "And I can catch birds and lizards and such. We do not lack. We can provide for ourselves."

She turned away and Bala walked back to his house, having been dismissed.

Still every day he watched them and wondered about them and why they were here. Such a woman, an old brave woman—for courage stood in every line of her face—such a woman must be here for some purpose. She had come here not because she must but because she wanted to.

And why had she brought her grandson with her? To provide her with food and skins and shelter? No, such an old woman would prefer taking her chances on dying alone or living on her own resources.

There must be some other reason why the boy was with her.

Bala wondered and wondered, and was glad to have something to wonder about. Was pleased to wake in the mornings and see the two small figures moving about among the great leg bones of long-dead beasts, two other human beings here in this valley with him for whatever mysterious purpose.

He watched the grandson go off with his spear and come back with food. He watched the old woman making a fire and cooking their meals and treating the skins of deer and hare.

They too slept outside, for the weather was warm and pleasant, and Bala supposed the others must feel, as he had done at first, uneasy about sleeping in their house of bones.

When bad weather forced them all to sleep inside, Bala noticed a curious thing. When the old woman emerged after the rain was over, she danced. She stamped and leaped and twisted; her long hair and tattered clothes flew about her like the branches of a storm-tossed tree.

Bala did not like to watch. She danced for some design of her own making, secret and important. He was intruding when he watched. But he could not turn his eyes away and watched until she stopped at last and stood for a long time with bowed head.

With all his heart Bala longed to know her. Still he waited. He dared not be the one to come forward.

And then one day when Bala was stalking a deer, he came face to face with the grandson. The boy must have been hunting the same deer and somehow they had not seen each other, so intent was each on his prey, until they were almost upon one another.

The boy was big, though not yet full grown. He was well made and handsome, and his clothes, unlike his grandmother's, were clean and whole and tidily kept.

Only his eyes bothered Bala, for there was, far in their

depths, something sly and more than sly, dangerous and fearsome. Like his grandmother this boy had great courage, but unlike her he did not know the proper way to use it.

Or he did not want perhaps to use it in the proper way.

Now he smiled, but whatever dwelt deep inside him did not go away with the smile. It stayed there still, cold and hard and somehow more fearsome because of the smile.

"We have both lost our quarry," he said, for the deer had bounded away.

"There are more deer," answered Bala. "And hares and rabbits and birds."

The boy nodded indifferently. "We do not need food anyway," he continued. "I hunt because there is little else for me to do. My grandmother can spend her hours sitting in the sun and be happy. But I am young and must move about. Better the company of hares than the company of an old woman who would rather speak to her memories than to me."

Bala was moved to ask the boy to hunt with him. He too longed for companionship and a way to occupy his days.

Yet he recalled the old woman's words. She had spoken the truth, he was sure. It was best that she and this boy not be his friends or even his neighbors for a time.

"My name is Bala," he said at length. "If you need my help, you have only to ask."

The boy smiled again. "I am Medana and my grandmother is called Kotil," he said.

And Bala went away, as though he must hunt further.

After that he sometimes saw the boy raise his arm in greeting in the mornings. The boy and the old woman watched him too, then, and wondered why he was here.

One evening not many days later the old woman came to Bala's campfire.

"I see you keep well," she said. "I am glad." She paused. "I see that you do not want to say why you are here or how long you mean to stay. I do not want to press you. But I have come to tell you why I am here, for I have watched my grandson hail you in the morning, and sooner or later he will find a way to meet you again, when I cannot prevent the meeting. Someday when you travel north to the trees he will follow you. Or he will go before you and wait for you to come to him."

She stopped once more and stared into the fire. Bala could see that she was reluctant to say what she had to say.

"There is something the matter with my grandson. I do not know what it is," she went on. "It is an evil that lives inside his head. He does not do bad things himself. It is rather that he makes others do bad things. He has a way. He knows how to give another person the notion to do what he or she should not do, so that other person must take the blame. I have come here with him, for I know a little magic and I am trying to cure him.

If I cannot cure him, at least I will keep him from harming others. That is why I have brought him here. I have made a chain between him and me, a strong chain. He can wander, but he cannot leave me. Still he can reach you. I give you this warning. Whatever your reason for being here, do not let him discover it."

Bala knew then that Kotil herself had learned in some way why he was here. She knew that he was a man who had lost his honor and with it his family and friends.

She knew that he longed to be once more at home with the people he loved, to have life be as it had once been for him. And that he must use all his strength to put those longings from his heart.

And in turn he sensed something about Kotil. He knew why she did her strange dance. She could not spend a night shut up with Medana's evil without running a risk of being defiled by it. Therefore on those mornings she danced away the bad effects of having spent long hours imprisoned with her grandson.

Bala knew that magic dances were very powerful and he had heard often how they could be used to cleanse and purify. He was again ashamed that he had watched her dance, a ritual which she should have been allowed to perform in privacy.

Now he said, "I am grateful for your warning. I will heed it."

She went away and that day Bala did not hunt but sat by his house and pondered.

And in the next few days he kept a diligent watch and

often saw Medana following him or waiting for him a long way ahead. Bala no longer walked to the forests at the northern head of the valley, not simply because he was afraid of meeting Medana, but because the year was growing dry and hot. In the woodlands the leaves hung limp upon the trees and the birds seldom sang or even showed themselves.

Hunting became a real task, not something done to pass the time but something done because birds and hares were scarce, and once or twice Bala went supperless to bed.

He hunted now farther and more intensely than he had before, and it was thus that he forgot Kotil's warning and allowed Medana to find him, waiting for rabbits, crouched in the grass; in grass now turned brown and dry, so crisp it crackled underfoot and made hunting even more difficult.

Yet Medana was able to come silently up to him. Bala had observed before that Medana could move as quietly as a shadow.

"I have killed a deer," Medana announced. "We will share it with you, if you like."

Bala hesitated. He was hot and weary and would have liked some of the deer meat. Yet he answered, "No, I will soon have my rabbits. You and your grandmother will need all the meat of your deer for yourselves. I thank you."

"Very well," Medana said. He smiled and gave a small

shrug. "You have been talking to my grandmother, I believe, for you have done your best to avoid me. I know. I have seen you turn aside when I came near."

Bala said nothing to this. He could not deny it.

Medana went on. "She has told you that she believes I am evil person. Now I will tell you something about my grandmother. She speaks the truth, for she has taken a vow that she will never lie. And if you ask her any question, she must tell you the truth if she knows it. It was a very solemn vow."

"Then you are an evil person and she was right to warn me against you," said Bala abruptly.

"So she believes," Medana answered. He smiled again and went away.

By long effort Bala killed two grouse for his supper. He went back to his house and turned over in his mind what Medana had told him.

The next day he determined to go once more to the north forests. Surely he could find a deer there if he climbed high enough into the hills. There would still be much forage under the branches of the great trees and there would still be water in the streams. No doubt many had fled there and Bala would follow.

He set out early and made certain that Medana did not see him go. He kept a careful watch and saw no sign of the boy.

It was a long journey and at its end the shade of the trees was welcome and the long slope of the hills urged him farther and farther in among them, toward the peaks where the giant snake Ulukini lay hidden.

Was it true? Did one last, enormous serpent lie somewhere among those distant ridges?

Bala turned back quickly and, when he had killed his deer, left the forest hurriedly, not glancing back. Medana was waiting for him at the edge of the valley and walked with him.

"I have not killed anything for my grandmother and me to eat today," Medana said. "It is good that we still have some of the meat from the deer."

"Yes," answered Bala. "Though I am ever willing to share with you anything that I have."

"And we with you," murmured Medana.

They walked on and Medana asked, "Have you lived here always?" and Bala answered, "Almost always."

For it was almost so. His life in the village he had put behind him and he did not think of it if he could avoid it.

"Would you not like to go back there, where you came from?" Medana pressed him. "You must be far from where you were born. I am sure it is so. I asked my grandmother and she said it was so. She is old and wise and knows much. And she must always speak the truth."

Bala walked on but at last he said, "This is where I live now."

And he hastened his steps and left Medana behind.

Yet he turned his head once and looked back up at

the mountains where the last giant snake lay sleeping in the sun. Perhaps.

And time went by.

The drought was long and hard, and one day the old woman and the boy came with a leather bottle and Kotil requested some water to drink, for their own spring had grown muddy and foul.

Though the spring near Bala's hut no longer bubbled up strongly, the water was still fairly clean and fresh. He filled their bottle and handed it to the old woman. "The rain is not far off," he told her. "I think we will soon have rain."

She shook her head. "No," she told him. "There will be no rain till days have passed more than the fingers of my two hands. We will have to do with what we have, with your help."

Medana gave his grandmother a cunning look. He turned suddenly and stared northward toward the hills. Bala followed his glance.

"There will be water in the hills, high up," Bala said. "Perhaps I could travel there and fetch some back for us."

"It is best not to travel in the hills," answered Kotil sharply. "There are many spirits in the hills and some of them dislike humankind and do not want our presence among them."

She turned away, but Bala took her arm.

"I have heard that one last great snake, Ulukini, one

of those who bear a magic crystal in the skull, lives up in the mountains. Is it true?" he asked.

Kotil gave Bala and Medana both a sullen look.

"Yes, is it true," she answered finally. "The last great snake."

She and Medana walked back to their house and Bala watched them go and a plan formed in his mind. Or not a plan, a thought for making a plan. It worried him, and in the nights throbbing with heat he lay awake and stared at the hazy stars and talked with himself as though he were two different people, with different views and feelings and even lives.

The dry weather continued, as Kotil had said it would, and Bala's spring dwindled. At last he arose one morning and walked to Kotil's house.

"My spring will soon be gone," he told her. "It is scarcely more than a trickle. If you will lend me your leather bottles, I will go into the hills and bring back enough water for us to drink until the rains come. Otherwise we may die."

Kotil stared at him strangely, but she brought out her three leather bottles. Bala had not thought to make one for himself, although he dressed his deerskins with as much care and skill as if he was intending to sell them in the market place. His wife, when he had a wife, had made their bottles and he was not sure he possessed the craft and quickness of hand to do it himself.

"Do not go too far," Kotil warned him. "And be very careful. Watch all you do."

"I will be careful," Bala promised.

He took the bottles and set out. He walked quickly though the day was hot and no wind stirred across the valley. When he came to the forest, he went at once to a place where he had, earlier in the year, found a small stream.

The stream was dry now and the moss on the stones had turned black and the ferns had died. He followed the dry bed up and up, and soon there was a little moisture among the rocks. And then a little higher a tiny rill.

He climbed and climbed and at last came to a real brook, and not much farther on to the source of the brook, a spring tumbling out from between two stones.

Bala set his bottles down at that spot. He drank and the water was sweet and cool. And then he went on.

There was no sign that any man had ever been here before, and he left a trail of sorts by which to find his way back quickly—a broken twig, a little pile of pebbles, a knife mark on a tree trunk.

But there was no sign either of the great snake Ulukini and at last he turned back.

He found the bottles and filled them and carried them as carefully as he could down the hillside and out of the forest. Kotil and Medana came to meet him.

"You have been gone a long time," said the old woman.

"Yes," answered Bala. "The spring was far up in the ridges. And I traveled back slowly. I did not want to drop the bottles. As it is, I have not brought back a great deal of water."

"It will suffice," said Kotil. "In two days we will have some rain and then in another two days much rain, more than we will want."

Bala did not look at the old woman, for he knew she would see in his eyes the reason he had been gone so long. She was a very wise woman, and no doubt she would know all he had been thinking during the sleepless nights when he had watched the stars and found himself two people warring one against the other.

"Did you see any signs of the spirits who live among the ridges?" asked Medana. "The ones my grandmother warned you about?"

"I saw nothing," Bala answered honestly.

"Did you see signs of the great serpent?" Medana's voice was mocking.

"I saw nothing," repeated Bala. He picked up one of the bottles and with it returned to his house.

The old woman had predicted rightly. In two days there were showers and then in another two days rain and rain, unending, endless.

And then there was a calamity. The house of Medana and Kotil, not so well built and sturdy as Bala's, collapsed. Bala saw it happen, saw the bones slowly slide away and topple. He ran at once and pulled the old woman from the wreckage and helped her to her feet. She was not injured, only a little frightened.

Medana was not inside, having gone to look at a trap

for hares which he had set some days before. When he returned, he and Bala searched the ruins for the leather bottles and some skins.

"We will have to live together in Bala's house," said Kotil reluctantly. "The rain will end soon and we will rebuild our house."

It was crowded for three people in Bala's small shelter. There was little to eat and no dry wood for a fire. Kotil sang most of the day in a low, sad murmur and Bala thought she must do it to keep Medana's evil at bay, for she could not do her dance.

Bala himself often walked in the pouring rain rather than sit crushed together with the others in the house of bones, listening to the old woman's cracked voice going on and on. Sometimes Medana came with him. They would walk the length of the valley and back, looking for birds and rabbits. They found no great plenty, but enough.

And at last the weather changed and the sun shone once again and a steamy heat rose from the earth.

But before that happened the damage had been done. Two nights before the rain ended, Bala came back to his house with a hare from Medana's trap and enough twigs and grass to build a smoldering fire to cook the hare. Medana was pleased that his snare had succeeded at last and Kotil was glad of the fire, however small. Her bones ached from the damp.

Only Bala was discontent, sorry that Medana and not he had supplied the meal, sorry that he must share his house and the smoky air with this lean old woman and her grandson. Perhaps he had grown overaccustomed to living alone.

That was how the evil slipped in, he knew later. When he had allowed himself to be angry and troubled and fretted by little and foolish things, then even Kotil's songs and charms could not protect him. Medana must have known the moment had come.

"Today when I was out," Medana said suddenly, "the sun broke through the clouds. For just a breath it lit the mountain tops. Tell us, Grandmother, about the spirits there and what would happen to someone who climbed to the places where they stay."

"They are not to be spoken of lightly," she answered and her voice was curt. "And I know little about them, simply that they are there and some are good to humans and some are not, and if one goes among them one must go with care and protect oneself as best one can."

"Then tell us about the giant snake Ulukini and the wonder-working stone in its head," Medana urged in his sly voice.

Kotil sighed, rubbing her knees.

"Everyone knows," she said. "Seven of them were created. Seven giant serpents, each with a marvelous crystal in its head. They came into the world at its very beginning and they were meant to live until the world should end. Men have killed six of them and now there is only Ulukini left."

"How could they live until the end of the world?"

asked Bala. "If men can kill them, cannot other things destroy them?"

"No," she replied. "Only men can find the one vulnerable spot. Only men have the knowledge to kill them and the sharp spear points which can be used against them."

Medana did not look at Kotil. He kept his eyes on Bala, and at last Bala asked, "What is the spot where the spear can enter?"

Kotil gazed into the fire for a long time. And then she said sadly, "Behind the head. Between the third and fourth row of scales. But it is wicked to speak of such things. The last great snake Ulukini is safe upon its mountaintop and should remain so."

She seized Medana by his chin and turned his head so that he must stare into her eyes or drop his lids. "Know this. The blood of the giant snake is poisonous," she cried harshly. "Should anyone thrust his spear into that vital spot, the blood would gush forth and he would die!"

Bala was astonished. How had Gatani's grandfather escaped such a fate? He must have been clever as well as brave. Bala was not clever or brave.

Medana did not turn his eyes from his grandmother's. He stared boldly and smiled his small smile and said softly, "Six of the great snakes have been killed, Grandmother. There must be a way."

And the sun shone at last and the grass grew green once again. Bala lived once again alone in his house.

He did not go to help Kotil and Medana rebuild their shelter and they came no more to ask for water from his spring or any other thing. And Bala was lonely once more and without much to occupy his hands or his heart and so he spent long hours looking up into the mountains and wondering. And his thoughts went ever and again to the great serpent Ulukini and the stone in its head.

He reminded himself that he was neither brave nor clever.

The days had begun to shorten. Bala woke one morning before light. He rose and took his spear and his knife and some hides and a little food and set out toward the north, toward the forested ridges. As when he had left his wife and children he had tried not to look behind, so now he tried not to look ahead.

He remembered Kotil's words about the unfriendly spirits in the ridges. He had no weapon against them. He stopped and almost turned back, for his fear was great. And in the end he made himself go forward and thought only about walking, putting one foot in front of the other and walking and walking.

When he came into the forest, he followed the stream, now full and gushing, where he had got water in the dry season. He found beyond it some of the traces he had made for himself at that time. By nightfall he was far above the point he had reached before and lay down and slept where weariness overcame him.

In the morning he was hungry and ate what he had

brought with him, for he was afraid of killing any of the birds or animals he saw in the undergrowth. Who knew whether such killing might not anger the spirits around him? Who knew indeed anything about these tall peaks and the dark trees which grew along them or what he might do to offend the invisible beings which lived among them?

He began to climb again, and as the day went on and all he saw seemed not so different from what he had seen in other mountain forests, he made up his mind not to tremble as he had trembled before. Whatever befell him, befell him, and since he could not foresee it, he would try not to fear it but simply wait for it to happen.

And nothing happened.

He climbed up and down the ridges, always going higher when he could. And that evening he killed a hare for his supper and built a fire, and when he had eaten, polished his spear as had always been his custom. If any spirit wished to harm him, it could find him at any time, in daylight or in darkness. And so he slept and no harm came to him.

Once in a while as he journeyed he had a curious sensation of being surrounded by watching eyes. Did these beings know why he had come? And did they know that a terrible fate awaited him? And did they stay their own fury against him because there was no need, since he was destined to die a dreadful death?

He shook away such notions. All woodlands were filled with watching eyes.

For three days he climbed and searched for signs of the great snake Ulukini. Ulukini was there, somewhere, Kotil had said so. But perhaps Bala was not the one meant to discover it. The thought was a happy one. He need not risk death by poison. And yet he went on searching.

And one morning he climbed the highest ridge he had yet come to and looked down into a little saddle in the hills—and there it lay. Ulukini, the last great snake.

He almost cried out in amazement. He had not known it would be so gigantic, lying coiled in a pile taller than a man. Its body was thicker than the bodies of two men and its head was vast.

What he had not known either was that Ulukini was so beautiful. In the morning sun its scales glittered, gold and green and shining blue and purple. The colors moved in waves, the patterns rippled along its back and sides, glowing here, dimming there, but always alive with a cold and vivid fire. Bala caught his breath in his throat. He had not dreamed of such a sight.

For a long time he stared down in wonder. And then he remembered. He had not come to admire. He had come to make a plan and try to carry it out.

He surveyed the snake and its surroundings carefully. This must be where the monster lived and slept. The ground was worn and bare of vegetation—no trees, no brush, no grass. Several wide paths led away from the spot and into the forest. When Ulukini went in search of food or water—and Bala did not know whether it required food or water, being so nearly immortal—no doubt it followed one of these paths.

In a space he discovered this was true, for the great snake roused itself, weaving its huge head back and forth, unwreathing itself from its heap of gleaming coils, and then sliding lithely off among the trees along one of the paths.

Whether it went for food or drink Bala could not know.

For two days Bala watched the giant snake. He learned about the times of its comings and goings, and that it did not see well but used other senses to guide it, touch and smell and hearing.

Bala went away, for he had made a plan and now must try to carry it out. He killed two animals he did not generally kill, for their flesh was not flavorful, but they were very fat. He scraped the fat carefully into one of the hides he had brought with him, and then he sought something else.

He was fortunate and found it almost at once, quartz stone, that rock which is composed of shining crystals.

He pounded up the rock and added the bright particles to the fat and stirred them together well. He made a sort of bag of the hide and tied the mouth tightly with tough grasses.

Then he returned to Ulukini's lair. He concentrated on each step of his plan and tried to carry it out carefully and not let himself consider failing. Or at any rate not let himself care whether he failed.

The Last Great Snake · *67*

One of the great snake's trails sloped away to the west. Bala waited until Ulukini had disappeared along another of its paths, and then he went a short way down the western slope. Using his knife and his hands, he dug a deep and narrow trench. He spent a long time at this task, and when he heard Ulukini returning, the day was nearly over.

Bala went swiftly away and hid himself among the trees and in the darkness polished and sharpened his spear and his knife.

He lay down but he could not sleep. He was afraid to sleep. He was afraid to think lest he think of failing and what would happen to him. He lay and looked up at the forest roof above him and tried to think of nothing at all, and then he fell asleep.

He woke and jumped to his feet, believing he had missed his opportunity. But it was still midnight-dark and he had not slept long.

He spent the time till dawn in misery, turning his mind this way and that, away from the happy past and the strange present and the unknown and foreboding future.

And then the night began to dissolve slowly, trees and bushes became shadows and the spaces between them something lighter than shadow. He let himself think of his plan, going over and over it until he was sure of just what he meant to do and how to do it.

When the light grew strong enough so that he could see plainly, he undid his flask full of fat and quartz and rubbed it carefully over his body. He stood under the trees nearly naked and glistening even in the twilight.

He took his spear and his knife and went softly, softly up the western trail. When he came to the narrow trench he had dug the day before, he stopped. The sun was coming up but was not yet high enough to shine upon him. He waited quietly, taking small, shallow breaths.

He could see above him the shadow of Ulukini coiled asleep at the top of the rise. And then the sun climbed a little higher in the sky and the time had come. The rays fell upon him and he shone like a burning tree. Ulukini would be dazzled, its half-blind eyes would never find this glaring object in the glaring light of daybreak.

Bala shouted, "Ulukini! Oh, giant snake, come here!" He called as loudly as he could and saw the serpent's head raised and the long forked tongue come darting out of the great mouth.

"Come here!" cried Bala. He danced back and forth behind the trench, a brilliant firefly of a man in the red and brilliant light of dawn.

The serpent appeared at the top of the slope, hissing in anger, and the long beautiful body flowed toward him, and Bala's heart beat fast. And still he danced and called.

And when the huge beast was almost upon him, its head almost over the trench, he sprang forward and with all his strength plunged his spear behind the head, between the third and fourth row of scales. In one gesture he freed his weapon and leaped back. He ran far down the slope and stopped and looked up.

He heard the beast utter a long, whispering groan, saw it writhe and slash feebly through the air and then go still.

Was it over then? So quickly and simply? He had truly killed Ulukini, the last great snake? He went slowly back the way he had come and saw that the snake was in fact dying.

The great body quivered faintly and blood gushed from its mouth and from the wound and poured into the trench Bala had dug. The blood smoked and hissed, he could hear it burning down and down into the earth, harmlessly vanishing into the dark depths and rocks.

And while he watched a dreadful thing happened. The colors dimmed along Ulukini's scales, the iridescence faded and went out like the embers of a smoldering fire. The snake was gray and dull and then the body itself began to dwindle and collapse, as a burnt log collapses into ashes.

Within a few minutes nothing remained of the giant snake Ulukini and its marvelous beauty but a twisted ridge of dust. Even the vast head had shrunk and the eyes fallen in and the skull crumbled. Bala could see the shape of the magic stone revealed in the top of the skull.

He could not move. He could only stand and stare. He had thought to do a brave and clever thing and he had merely done a deed full of horror that nothing could undo. Ulukini the last great snake had gone to earth and never again would sunlight or moonlight glisten on those cold rainbow scales. Of all that wonder and loveliness there was now simply this small heap of grime.

After a long while Bala roused himself. He went close to the snake and gazed at the shape of the magic crystal embedded in what was left of the skull. The stone was his by right and yet for a long time he could not make himself reach down and claim it.

Let Ulukini keep it. He would have left it save that he knew someone else would surely find it and he would have done this deed in vain. He took his knife and slid it around the stone—and one tiny last drop of blood flew out and fell upon his forearm.

He was protected by the layer of fat, yet the venom burned into his arm. Frightened, he picked up a handful of dirt and grass and rubbed and rubbed at the spot, but the burning went on.

He was to die then. He had truly killed the snake to no purpose, for now the snake was killing him. He squatted and waited to die, here in this far place by the ruins of mystery and legend.

But he did not die. The burning stopped, and when he looked at his arm, the blood was gone. Only in its place a tiny replica of Ulukini clung to his skin, an infinitesimal snake of green and silver and blue and purple, no bigger than a moth's antenna.

So he would not die, only bear forever the mark of what he had done. He went on with the work he had started and lifted the stone from the skull.

He scarcely dared look at it but carried it away at

once into the forest and wrapped it gently in moss and leaves. Then he went back to his sleeping place of the night before and gathered up his few belongings and set out for the valley.

He hurried, for now summer was truly gone and the leaves above his head were beginning to turn color. He had no wish to spend another winter in his house of bones.

He had not left a trail for himself as he had traveled to find Ulukini, but like all good hunters he knew where he was going and how to get there. So it did not take many days before he found himself on the last far slopes of the northern mountains and saw the drying grasses of the valley and the strange bones and then at last his house.

Smoke rose from the hole in the roof and he knew Kotil and Medana had taken over his shelter and he was glad. It was a sign that he should not linger here but travel on at once.

Kotil had sensed his coming and they stood waiting for him.

"We took your house," said Kotil when she had greeted him. "Our second shelter was even weaker than our first and fell of its own weight. We did not know that you would be returning. We are grateful for the use of this one. I will see that it is properly cleansed for you."

Bala shook his head. "It is no matter. The house is yours now. I do not intend to stay here again," he told her.

Kotil looked at him sharply and sadly. "You have done it then?" she asked in a quiet voice.

Bala did not meet her eyes. "I do not know what you mean," he said. He was ashamed of his pretence. Stealthily he touched the little image of the snake on his arm.

"And now you can return," Kotil made a statement rather than a question of the words.

"And now I can return," Bala responded. The three of them stood in silence. Bala thought back over it all, the arrival of the two strangers and Kotil's warning about Medana.

"There is this, Kotil," Bala said at last. "It was not Medana's doing only. The notion was there in my mind all along. Medana merely helped me find it. He could not make me do a thing I knew already I was going to do. It was I who lacked the strength to resist."

"A notion in the mind is one thing," the old woman answered sharply. "Learning how to do a thing and doing it are other things entirely. I should not have stayed here with Medana. But I believed I could protect you."

And Bala remembered how Medana had mocked him and challenged him until Bala could not resist asking Kotil to affirm that Ulukini dwelt in the hills and to tell how it might be killed. He remembered the evening when he and Kotil and Medana had sat around the fire in his house and he, Bala, had been angry and resentful and had let Medana slip into his head the determination to listen to only one of those two people arguing in his mind, the determination to seek out and kill Ulukini.

If he had been strong enough . . . if Kotil had taken Medana away . . . if Bala had gone away himself . . . .

"I could not protect you," Kotil said sorrowfully. "It may be that I cannot protect anyone from Medana, but only keep him here, away from everyone, where he can do no further harm."

But Kotil was an old woman. The chain that bound Medana to her would grow weaker. Soon enough he would go back into the world of other people.

Bala looked once again into Medana's eyes. Only death would extinguish the little cold slippery thing that lived in their depths. But because of his nature death would come for Medana sooner than for other young men. What harm he would do he had better do quickly. Soon he would be the victim of his own mischief. He would meet an evil stronger than his own and it would turn on him and kill him.

Bala said nothing of his thoughts. Instead he bade them good-bye and wished them well and began the long walk to his home.

And time went by.

The journey back took much more time than it had taken Bala to reach the valley of strange bones. The weather turned cold and there was often rain or even snow. And Bala had now in his keeping a magic crystal, so he traveled always away from paths and trails. He did not know whom he might meet who could discern the stone's presence and try to take it away from him.

And he went with care in order not to offend the stone and gave it frequently water from the clearest springs he could find and sometimes a drop or two of deer's blood. He did not know how properly such things were done, but he did them as well as he could and asked the stone over and over to forgive him for his clumsiness and ignorance.

In its nest of moss and leaves the stone continued to glow and flash and he assumed that it was pleased.

It was good that he had the stone to tend, for the slowness of his journey pricked him and made him impatient, and he could not keep himself from thinking of his wife and children and the chance that he might once more be with them. Only the care of the stone kept his mind from such thoughts.

And at last he was among hills and streams he recognized and he went more swiftly, though still keeping himself hidden. And on the day he reached his village it was almost dark and he waited, sleepless, till morning before he entered the town.

He waited till the day was well begun and most of the people gathered in the market place. He walked then openly and firmly into their midst. He went straight to Gatani and put into the other man's hands the moss within which lay the shining crystal.

"I have brought you a magic stone," said Bala. "To replace the one you have lost."

Gatani stared at Bala and then looked down into his

hands. Carefully, with his thumb, he brushed away the moss until the stone glowed forth. Gatani sprang to his feet.

"So!" he cried scornfully. "You have grown weary of exile and have returned my magic stone to me! You have brought back my magic stone!"

Bala could not speak. That he should have done and endured all that he had done and endured and have it come to this: That Gatani should still accuse him of theft and dishonor.

He staggered as if from a blow and from shock he could not speak. He heard sounds of disapproval from those around him and saw their hostile looks, but in a kind of daze.

He raised his hand and caught Gatani's arm and steadied himself and found his voice.

"This is not your stone!" he shouted and heard how fierce, how hoarse with fury was the sound of his own words. "To get this stone I killed the last great serpent, Ulukini. I give it to you freely, to replace your stone. But it was I who killed the snake and I who bear the mark of its death."

He extended his forearm and pointed to the tiny snake there.

Gatani leaned forward. "I see no mark," he said at last. And he called for two elders of the village, who served as priests, to come forward and look.

"We see no mark," they repeated. "Besides it is not possible that the last great serpent is dead."

Bala touched the little snake wonderingly. Was it true? Could no one see the brand except himself? He should not have concealed it from Kotil. She perhaps might have seen it or told him why it would be hidden from others.

And now he stood among those who had once been his friends, and considered that he had done a dreadful thing for no reason at all. He was not to regain the love of his family or the respect of his townsmen.

He raised his eyes to Gatani's.

"Ask the stone," he said furiously. "I dare you to ask the stone itself whether I robbed you of your magic crystal and whether this is it."

Gatani frowned. He was afraid of the stone and of asking it questions. Yet he could not refuse what Bala asked and he knew it.

"It will take two days," he said after a while.

"I have been gone nearly two years," Bala replied. "I can wait another two days."

"Very well," agreed Gatani. He went away carrying the stone and the elders went with him to see that all was done properly.

Bala's wife came to his side and put her hand on his arm and he went with her to their house. And for those two days she did not leave him to work in her garden or go to the market place.

They said little to each other of the nearly two years which were gone and could not be recalled, for there was little to say. Bala's children had grown so that he scarcely recognized them and they did not remember him. Yet he saw no way to change things and spoke to them as a father would and held them in his arms.

Bala's wife said she saw the tiny snake on his forearm, but when he asked her to touch it, she put her finger on the wrong spot and he knew she had lied to comfort him, because she loved him.

And the two days came to an end. Gatani came into the market place with the elders and stood before all the people.

In two days Gatani had grown old, for it is a trying and dangerous thing to look into the depths of a magic crystal and see the truth. The truth may crack a heart.

Gatani spoke and everyone listened with care.

"This magic stone is not my magic stone," he said. "Bala did not steal my stone. My stone grew angry with me, so angry that it swallowed itself. I do not know how I offended it. Perhaps I gave it too much deer's blood or too little. Or perhaps there was something I should have done and failed to do without knowing. Whatever happened, Bala did not take my stone and I accused him wrongly. This is the magic crystal from the head of the last giant snake, Ulukini."

A man called out, "Ah, you are not worthy to own the stone and look into its depths!"

And many people nodded and looked coldly at Gatani. And Bala stepped up beside him and motioned that he had something to say and everyone listened.

"Once I was a man of honor and I lived in this village," he said. "I have been away for nearly two years. Now I am come home and am once again a man of honor. I did not come home in order that another man should go away and take my place in loneliness and disgrace. Gatani was in error, but he acted as he thought he must. He did not then know the truth. I have brought him another stone. It is his and he must decide whether it shall take the place of the one given him by his grandfather."

"This is so," said one of the elders. "What Bala has said is right and as it should be."

And Gatani took his place again in the market and was treated as he had always been. But everyone saw that Gatani had changed. For though he knew he would never be an elder or a great hunter or storyteller or maker of spears, yet he had always walked with pride because his grandfather had chosen him to receive the magic stone. Now he walked with bent head and seldom spoke and was older than his years.

And what became of the stone from the head of Ulu-kini no one knew except the elders, and they did not say.

So once more Bala lived in his house with his wife and his children and he spoke to them as a husband and father would. He taught his children songs and games and told them what was right to do. He hunted for meat and skins. His wife worked in her garden and helped Bala prepare the skins for sale in the market. Bala traded in the market and everyone came to trade with him and tell

The Last Great Snake · *79*

him where the hunting was good and who had a new baby and that a wolf had been seen near the town, and news of such sort.

And Bala was again a man of honor and happy to be once more at home with his family and friends.

Yet sometimes he went into the forest and sat alone and touched the tiny snake on his arm, that only he could see. He thought about honor and what it was and what it was worth. He thought of Kotil and Medana, and of Gatani.

But most of all he thought about Ulukini, the last great snake, and of its beauty and how its colors had once glistened in the sun and now would glisten no more.

And time went by.

DITA'S STORY

EVER SINCE she was five years old Dita had wanted to become a witch.

When Dita was five years old her mother lay dying of an unknown fever. Dita's father asked the village priest for help, but the priest refused. The priest said Dita's mother was a wicked woman and deserved to die, for twice he had seen her coming out of sacred places she should never have entered and once she had slapped her mother-in-law.

So Dita's father had taken much meat and many hides and all five of the beautiful river pearls he had found in his lifetime and traveled some distance to another town. He had paid all these things to the witch who lived in that town and she had returned to his house with him.

She had fed Dita's mother on brews and potions.

She had spoken many incantations in a low, guttural voice and made curious symbols in the air around the sick woman's bed.

And Dita's mother had recovered.

But more than that, marvelous as it was to Dita, the witch had taken a great interest in Dita, who was small for her age and had a weak and withered arm. The witch had talked to the little girl and showed her some of the strange things she carried in her witch's bundle and let her help in gathering certain herbs and roots.

So Dita made up her mind to become a witch. She told no one.

Three years later her mother was dead, killed by a tree falling on her as she was gathering nuts in the forest. The priest of the village pointed out that she had been a wicked woman and deserved to die.

Dita's father did not marry again but left her in the care of her two sisters, older than she. And though the sisters were good to her, Dita missed her mother.

After some time the sisters married, first one, then the other, and neither of them wished to bring Dita to live with her and her new husband. For she was still small and weak and had a wizened arm and was not much use in a household. Although she was willing and tried very hard, she could not dig in the garden very well or drive the beasts home from pasturing or carry heavy burdens.

She could tend the fire and cook, she could gather nuts and berries and fruits in the forest, but that was almost all. Her older sisters, though they loved her and were kind to her, did not believe their husbands should be asked to provide for one who could give so little in return.

Yet Dita's father was eager that she too should marry and leave home, for he felt that he was growing old and he wished to sit in the square with the other old men and be cared for by his sons-in-law and his nephews.

Dita secretly looked with favor upon one of the young men of the town, a man a little younger than she, who had already proven himself to be a wise man and a good hunter. It was not unusual for women of that village to marry men younger than themselves.

Still he was not yet of an age to marry and take on the care of a wife and family. More than that, he was strong and handsome and many girls besides Dita planned to be his wife.

Dita watched his comings and goings and promised herself that by the time he was old enough to marry she would be stronger and comelier and that she would be his choice. Her father had no such hopes and went about seeking someone to marry his daughter, someone who, for one reason or another, would not be particular or ask too many questions about Dita's skills or abilities.

And after some time he found such a one. A man came to ask permission to marry Dita, an old man who lived alone, far from the village. He was too old to care for his few beasts and his small garden alone. He had no children or close relatives. He did not like living in the town. Thus he wished to marry, now close to the end of his life, and have such help as a wife might offer.

He thought Dita could manage the tasks he would require of her, for they were not great. The two of them could dig the garden and herd the little flock and milk it.

Dita told her father that she did not wish to marry yet and certainly not an old man, who could not hunt and would be dead in a few years.

"The choice is not yours to make," her father told her. "I do not want to force you into marrying this man, but there is no other willing to have you. At least, when he dies you will have a house and a garden and some beasts. And he has a distant kinsman who brings him meat on occasion. No doubt the kinsman will feel some obligation to you when the old man dies."

Dita could see that her father was distressed for her. He was in truth growing old and wished to provide for her. It seemed to Dita that there must be some better way.

"Let us wait a while," she suggested. Perhaps in a while the old man would be dead or find someone else to marry.

Or someone else would want to marry Dita.

"Very well," her father answered. "We will wait two months. But no longer."

He looked gravely at his daughter. "I do not want to die without knowing that my youngest child has some possessions of her own," he said. "Your sisters and their husbands no doubt can help you in good times. But they have families of their own now, and in bad times they must put their families first. In bad times a woman alone, yet who has a house and a garden, can survive, at least."

What he said was true and still Dita did not want to marry the old man. Still she yearned to be the wife of Nogaro, the young man of her choosing. Two months was not a long enough time. It would be longer than that before Nogaro thought of marrying.

So Dita went to the priest.

The old priest, who had thought her mother a wicked woman, was dead. The new priest was a younger man, and tender-hearted. The ills and wickednesses of his people troubled him even more than they troubled those who suffered from them.

Whenever he looked at Dita he trembled for her future. Even more than her father, he worried over what would become of her.

Now he said, as brusquely as he could, for he wished always to hide his pity, "What is it that you want? A woman is ill and needs my attention, so do not bother me with trifles."

Dita was a little afraid, for though she suspected that he was a man who sympathized with her, she could not be sure, for he never spoke to her in any other way.

But what she had come about was no trifle. "Sir," she said quietly, "I wish to become a witch."

The priest stared at her in amazement. No one before had ever said such a thing to him.

Then he said, and now his voice was gentle, "Why would you want such a thing? The life of a priest or witch is hard. And all sorts of dangers lie in wait for them that other people never encounter. One must be very brave and strong to be a witch."

Then Dita was silent in her turn. She did not want to say what her true reasons were. She did not wish to say that she hoped to avoid marrying an old man and that she hoped to learn some charm that would make her a fit wife for Nogaro.

Nor did she want to tell him of the witch who had cured her mother—and how the old priest had disapproved, of the witch and of Dita's mother and of the cure. The new priest might not like hearing such things from her, though he must surely remember. All the village had known these things and had talked of them for many days.

At last Dita said, "I am brave. I am not strong, but I am brave. I have long wanted to be a witch and now the time has come."

The priest shook his head.

"We have never had a witch in our town," he pointed out. "I do not think the time has come. I cannot give you the knowledge you must have without a great deal of time and trouble. If I should take such time and trouble and then the village should not accept you, I would be filled with regrets. And so would you."

Dita stood for a while gazing down at the dust under

their feet. "But you could do it?" she asked finally. "If you were willing, you would know how?"

"Of course," he answered. "I am a priest. One does not get to be a priest without knowing such things."

Dita went away and in two months she married the old man. Before the marriage she dreamed strange, sorrowful dreams and woke in tears, but there was nothing she could do.

Her sisters comforted her when they saw how she grieved. "We will look after you," they promised.

But the old man lived a long way from the village. Her sisters would seldom see her and they would forget, having worries and troubles of their own.

And the day came and the old man arrived and took her away.

The house was dirty and full of spiders, his beasts were small but ill-tempered, and the garden was neglected and full of stones and weeds.

She chased out the spiders and tidied the house, and that she could do well enough. But she found it hard to manage the beasts, and when they strayed she was seldom able to bring them back and had to wait until they returned of their own accord.

And hoeing and tending the garden tired her very soon, so that she could work in it only an hour or two without sitting to rest for a long time. The old man was impatient with her and prodded her in the ribs when she grew weary and sat down to rest. He pinched her arms when she let the beasts stray.

He complained of the meals, which were bad, not because of Dita's cooking but because the vegetables from the garden were small and tough and flavorless and because the meat the kinsman sometimes brought them was old and half-rotted.

At night the old man made terrible noises in his sleep, blabbering and snoring so that Dita often went out of the house and slept in the open, though she was afraid with the forest too close around her and no other people near.

And at last one day she could bear it no longer. She left and walked back to her village and sought out her father, where he sat in the square with the other old men.

"Let me come home," she pleaded. "I cannot stay with him. Let me come home and I will keep your house and tend your garden till you die, and then I will die too."

Her father was saddened. He had thought she would grow resigned to her life with the old husband.

"I have given you to him," he told her seriously. "Unless he injures you or starves you or ties you to a post, I cannot take you back. Moreover, I have no house and garden now. It belongs to your elder sister and her husband, as is customary. And I sit in the square with the other old men and food is brought to us and we sleep where we will. You must return. A few pinches and prods cannot harm you, and he is too weak to do you any real hurt. In a day or two I will send one of your brothers-in-law to bring you some meat and help you in the garden. But more than that I cannot do."

And he looked at her with sorrow, for she seemed very tired and tears had reddened her eyes, and he thought perhaps he should not have let the old man marry her.

But what else had there been to do?

So when the old man came for her, Dita went back with him. And as they left the town Nogaro passed them and greeted them politely. But Dita did not answer and the old man only grunted, for he was furious that he had had to come again to the village to fetch his wife home.

In a few days Dita's second sister's husband came to their house and brought a young deer which he had killed. He stayed and sharpened the blades of the two hoes and helped Dita plant some new crops. He told the old man he must tether his beasts so that they could not run away from Dita.

Dita was sorry when he left. But the old husband was not sorry. He had not enjoyed having a young man tell him what to do.

When they were alone again, he pinched and prodded Dita more than ever. He laughed when her new crops were all destroyed by insects.

But when one of his beasts died, he did not laugh. He trembled with anger and blamed it on Dita, even though it was clear that the creature had died of old age and its own meanness.

After that each day became worse and worse and she grew wearier and wearier. And so one morning she did not go into the garden or to bring the little beasts out of their pen and take them to the grazing grounds.

Instead she walked into the forest and went on walking. It was quiet and cool, a bird sang somewhere far off, and the odor of fallen leaves and living leaves was sweet.

I will live here, thought Dita. I will live here in peace, for I will not stay any longer with that old man and his pinches and his rages. And I have no place to go, so I will find a hollow tree to sleep in and a spring to drink from. I will eat nuts and fruits and berries and the birds shall be my family and friends.

For she had always loved the songs of birds.

She wandered a long way, but as she did not know where she was going, she traveled almost in a circle and soon found herself close to the place where she had entered the forest.

She heard the old man calling for her and she ran in fear. She ran among the trees and bushes until she could go no farther. She saw a great fruit tree ahead of her and stumbled toward it, thinking she might climb up into its branches and hide.

Instead when she reached it, the ground beneath her feet suddenly gave way and she fell into a deep sinkhole between two big roots of the fruit tree. Her breath left her body and for a moment all was darkness.

Presently her lungs began to work again and she could see light coming down into the cave from the opening above her. And she thought herself safe. She did not believe the old man could find her here.

She shrank into the farthest corner of the hole and waited. She heard nothing and after a long while she was easy, sure that her husband had gone away, perhaps back to her village to search for her.

She looked about her then. The light was dim but she could see that the hole was not large, though it was very deep. There was a tiny spring at the bottom of one wall and she thought that perhaps at some time the water had gushed forth strongly and made this hollow in the earth.

She could not get out. The walls were far too high, and when she tried to climb them the soil crumbled under her hands and feet. She tried climbing up in many places and each time had to give up.

She was not frightened. When her husband did not find her in her father's village, he would come back to look for her and help her out. And then another time she could run away from him and plan more carefully how she would go and not fall into some hole.

But after some hours, when the day darkened and she knew that night would soon be upon the world, she grew afraid. Would some wild animal jump into the pit and kill her? Once again she cowered in the farthest corner.

The shadows grew deeper until she could see nothing at all. She heard the little spring whispering to itself and in the forest nightbirds called strangely and around her crickets whistled. She sat straining for the sound of paws or the snuffle of wolves, but nothing happened and at last she fell asleep.

When she woke it was daylight and she was terribly hungry. She drank the water of the spring and found a fruit which had fallen from the tree above her. She hoped that more would tumble in, but none did. So she pulled roots from the walls of her prison and chewed these. Surely someone would find her that day.

She waited as patiently as she could. Every now and then she was sure she heard the noise of approaching feet and she jumped up, crying out gladly. Each time she was disappointed and no one came.

And so one day passed and another and another. Once or twice she was certain someone walked by, and she called and called. But the walker either could not hear her or mistook her voice for some curious bird or insect and went by unheeding.

Hunters came this way often—one of them would surely hear her. The old husband would come for her. She would be glad to see even him. But no one came.

Dita was no longer afraid at night, for night and day were misery alike. Why had no one wanted to search for her? Why had everyone left her here in this dreadful place, dank and dim and cold as a grave? Was she to die here in truth?

She grew hungrier and hungrier with nothing to eat but an occasional fruit that dropped through the opening and the few roots she could claw out of the earth and now scarcely had the strength to chew. The nighttime crickets sometimes hopped close to her and she considered eating them, but she did not. It was not that she was repelled by the thought of eating insects, but that she had a certain fellow feeling for these small creatures, held captive here as she was and treated as indifferently by the world.

Why had not her father or her brothers-in-law or even her sisters come seeking her when the old man told them of her absence? Was she so worthless and so little loved? Was there no one to whom she mattered any longer?

She lost count of the days and grew weaker and weaker. And at last she made up her mind that indeed help was not forthcoming and she would die. She lay down on the floor of the pit and plastered her eyes shut with mud, for it was the custom among her people to close the eyes of the dead with earth. She placed her hands at her sides, palms downward, again according to the ways of her people.

And then she waited to die. It was the middle of the day and the birds were silent, and the crickets. Only the tiny spring whispered and whispered and whispered while Dita waited to die. . . .

But in the world above some women from Dita's village had ventured far into the forest gathering fruits and berries. One of them walked toward the great fruit tree through the roots of which Dita had fallen many days before.

The woman saw the gaping hole and wondered about it. Out of curiosity she walked quietly to it and peered into its depths. She could faintly see the body of a dead girl lying at the bottom of the hole, a small thin girl with her eyes covered with earth and her hands palms downward at her sides.

The woman was frightened and backed softly away and then ran to tell the others. "Come look!" she called. "A dead girl is lying yonder at the bottom of a hole."

The others were reluctant to see such a sight. It was not good to look upon the dead, especially one who lay dead in such a strange and unacceptable place.

"Send for the priest," said one of them. "He will know what to do."

And after some talk it was decided that three of the women should go and fetch the priest and the other three stay and watch the pit and its terrible contents.

Dita, lying on the earthen floor, heard nothing of this, only dimly the sound of the little spring, whispering and whispering. So when the priest, a while later, leaned over and saw her and cried out, "It is Dita!" she was too astonished to move.

And not until he had descended to the floor and touched her hand did she find the strength to sit up and scrape the mud from her lids and gaze up at him. The priest gave a great gasp of astonishment and fear and sprang away from her.

Those staring into the pit shouted in horror. "The dead girl is come alive! The dead girl moves!" Several of them ran away and would not look.

In the cave the priest touched Dita's cold arm timorously. "Dita," he said. "Is it you? Are you alive or dead?"

She could not answer. In truth she did not know. She had certainly thought herself dead.

"She cannot speak," the priest called up to the others. "We must lift her out."

So the men the priest had brought with him made a sort of chair of ropes and he raised her to her feet and placed her in it and the others pulled her up.

She could not stand and the full light of day dazzled her and she trembled violently. By and by she recovered herself somewhat, and still she did not speak. Her voice seemed to have left her and words swam through her mind without sense or order. The others stayed well away from her.

Then the men hauled the priest up from the pit. And again he touched her arm and spoke to her. He took some powder from his bundle and sprinkled himself with it, to ward off harm that might come to him from touching and speaking with a dead girl, and he sprinkled a little on Dita. He chanted a prayer to his guardian spirit, and then he felt safe.

He called to the others, "Bring food. For as she has been dead, she will not have eaten for a while, she will be hungry. And if she eats, we will surely know she is alive again."

One of the women came forward unwillingly and gave him some fruit and he in turn offered it to Dita. She took it in her quivering fingers and bit into it and then ate it all.

"You see," the priest exclaimed. "She has been dead and now is alive and eats like any living person!"

Still the others kept their distance.

"You need not fear," the priest told them. "I am here. If this is an evil thing which has happened, I can protect you. The evil will fall upon me and I will know what to do."

The others came closer then and looked at Dita with wondering eyes.

"Her husband's house is nearby," one of them said. "We should take her there and ask him how she came to die. Perhaps he placed her body in the hole instead of bringing her to the village to be buried properly. Perhaps that is why she came alive when the priest touched her. She thought he had come to see that she was buried as she should be."

"That may be so," the priest answered. "We will see."

One of the men picked Dita up and carried her to the old man's house. The priest walked beside him and kept his hand on the man's shoulder so that no ill could come to him from his mysterious burden.

The old husband was tending his garden. "Why have you brought this one here?" he asked angrily. "She ran away into the forest and would not come back. I no longer wish to have her for my wife. She is useless to me."

Dita understood what he said and for the first time in many days she was happy. Her father had not known she was missing and that was why he had not come searching for her. The old man had not considered it worth the trouble to make the long walk to the village to look for her or to tell her family she was gone.

He did not want her for a wife. Never again would he prod her or pinch her or screech at her in his wild way. She almost spoke, to say that she was glad. But still the words would not come to her properly and still she was not sure that she had not died and come back to life.

The priest questioned the old man. Had Dita been alive and well when he last saw her? Did he know anything about her death?

The old man shook his head. "What do you mean? She is not dead. She is there, alive."

The priest saw that he indeed knew nothing.

"You must come back to the village and give her back to her father," the priest said severely. "It was wrong not to come when she first ran into the forest."

They went away then in a long procession, leaving the old husband standing in his weedy garden. The men took turns carrying Dita, though she was no great weight, and the priest walked beside each one who carried her and warded off any danger that might come from this girl who had died and then come alive.

Her father was in the square with the other old men and when he heard what had befallen her, he was amazed.

"How did it come to happen?" he asked and the priest replied, "We do not know and she cannot tell us. But it is a strange and wonderful thing that has taken place."

"But what will become of her now?" asked her father. "If her husband gives her back to me, alas, I have no place for her. And this is not my daughter Dita any longer. One does not die and come back to life and remain the same person."

"That is likely true," agreed the priest. "And so I will take her to my home and care for her and see what person she has become. Perhaps we will discover how this has come about and then we will know what to do."

And he took Dita home with him.

His wife was not afraid and she fed and bathed this new person. She cried out when she saw how thin and frail the girl was.

"She is nothing but bones!" the priest's wife exclaimed. "She must have been dead many days."

"Perhaps," answered the priest. "But there is no harm in her. I have not felt the presence of any evil. We will care for her and see what happens."

The new person was grateful to be well cared for. She ate and grew strong and though she helped about the house and garden she was not asked to perform tasks beyond her strength. No one pinched or prodded her when she stopped to rest.

In the evenings the people of the village came to see her and talk to her and ask her about the time when she had been dead.

"I do not remember," she told them again and again. "I do not remember anything of when I was dead."

One man walked from another town because he had heard of the wonder and came to tell of another time when it had happened.

"My own grandfather died," he told the priest. "He

died in his home and was buried properly. But the next day he sat up in his grave and was alive again. And like this one he could not speak of what had happened to him."

"What did he become?" asked the priest, and the man replied, "Nothing. For in a week he was dead again and this time he did not come back to life. He lay in his grave and rotted with the other dead."

"It may be that will happen with this person," said the priest. "But I think not. For she grows stronger all the time, and speaks often, though she does not remember anything of her life before she died or of the time while she was dead."

And everyone was kind to her and no longer feared her but was glad that this happy thing had occurred, that a young and feeble girl had escaped from the hard cold grasp of death.

Still the priest knew that he could not keep her in his house forever. He must discover as soon as he could what person she had become and what was to be done with her.

So one day he took her by her hand and led her to a quiet place away from the village and spoke to her soberly. "The time has come for us to decide why you have died and come alive again," he told her and she nodded. "We must know what person you have become and what that person is to do."

He looked into her eyes for a long time. "Do you remember being Dita and being married to the old man who lives in the forest?"

After a while she answered honestly, "No." For she

had lived with the priest and his wife for many weeks and come to love them deeply and she felt that they loved her. She could no longer bear to think of the wretched days when she had been Dita, whose father had married her to an old husband, or of the prods and pinches the old man had given her and his terrible snore and his vile-tempered little beasts.

And most of all she could not bear to think of the long, hungry days and nights in the dark cave and her sorrow that no one cared enough to look for her and her fear of everything.

She could remember it, a little, if she wanted to and if she tried hard enough, but it all seemed something that had happened to someone else. So she could honestly say "No" to the priest's question.

"Then do you know what person you have become and why this thing has happened to you?" he asked.

And the new person thought for many minutes and finally she replied, "I do not know what person I am now. But this thing has happened to me in order that I may become a witch. That is what I believe."

The priest recalled that Dita too had once said she wished to become a witch.

"Perhaps that is true," he said. "There is much to be done in the town and I am sometimes in need of help. If you became a witch, you could help me. The people here think highly of you. But first I must visit all my sacred places and ask permission of their guardians. They will know if it is to be."

Thus it was decided that the new person had come to be a witch, if it was permitted. Every day the priest visited his holy places and implored their guardians for a sign, whether of pleasure or displeasure. When he came back to his house, he made no mention of these visits to anyone and especially not to the new person.

And she waited patiently and spoke with the people of the village, who treated her with friendliness and respect. They did not know what her plans were or what the priest was doing.

And after some time the priest again took her hand and led her to that quiet place away from the town.

"I have been to my sacred places," he told her, "and all their guardians have sent me messages that you should undergo the training that a witch must undergo. But I warn you that it is a long and wearisome process. You may fail and then I cannot help you."

"What will become of me if I fail?" asked the new person in a whisper.

"I do not know," responded the priest. "Perhaps you will die again. Or perhaps you will become once more only Dita."

It would be the same thing, the new person told herself. For the old husband had died recently and even if he were still alive, he would not want her. She would be without land or possessions and she would not matter to anyone and would likely perish in some time of hunger or drought or other peril.

And the new person was afraid and yet she was willing

to try, for it seemed to her to be a witch would be a good thing, as it had seemed to Dita.

Very soon she began to learn the things a witch must know. She learned how to make brews and potions and she learned songs and prayers to chant and the names of holy objects in a special language.

And this was only the beginning. She spent many hours alone in the forest, listening for the voices of the forest spirits and saying over and over the words that would make them happy and pleased with her.

She spent many hours in the village, walking with people and observing all the things they did that would make the spirits look with displeasure upon them, and searching all her own words and acts to see that she was no better than the men and women around her. For the things they did which troubled their invisible guardians, she herself often did too.

And all these deeds were done in secrecy, for the village must not know that the new person was learning to be a witch.

And after some time the priest sent her away into the gray land between living and dying. He took her into the forest and gave her a drink of many ingredients and by and by she went away into the gray land.

At first she saw nothing but grayness, as though a dense fog had fallen over the world. But gradually her sight cleared and things came rushing at her, things she did not know existed and could not afterwards have described to anyone, not even the priest. Shapes and colors of kinds she had never seen before danced before her eyes. And then there was again gray fog, and when it cleared she saw once more the witch woman who had cured her mother, and the banks of the river where her father had found his beautiful river pearls, and the old village priest.

And then she saw Dita being pinched and prodded by the old man and the sight made her want to weep with rage and pity. In the gray land, however, mortals must not move or weep or cry out. They must simply go as a cloud goes with the wind. And she was strong and did not cry out or weep.

She saw the great fruit trees among the roots of which she had fallen into the pit and seeing it frightened her horribly for a reason she could not understand. But she was brave and did not scream.

She drifted on and on, and the things she saw became more and more terrible and fearsome and the effort not to move or cover her eyes made her wearier and wearier, and when she thought she could bear it no longer, must leave and come back to the real world no matter what befell her, the priest touched her hand as he had when she lay dead at the bottom of the sinkhole, and she came out of the gray land and into daylight and warmth and the sound of birdsong.

"You are brave and strong," the priest said. "For I was with you part of the time, and it was a most terrible ordeal."

And the new person was pleased and smiled at his words, for she knew she had been brave and strong.

And some days later when she was recovered, the priest told her, "Now there is but one thing left to do. It is not difficult, but it is important. If it is not done, you cannot become a witch. And there is nothing you or I can do to make things happen one way or the other. For now you must be claimed by a spirit, who will give you true power. I do not know what that spirit will be and I can have no influence over which spirit chooses you or whether any does. If all the spirits refuse you, then you cannot be a witch."

And the new person trembled, but she followed the priest into the forest and sat where he told her to. And then he went away and she waited.

She waited two days and two nights and part of another day. She was not afraid in the darkness, even though once a wolf walked quite near, for the priest had protected her with a charm and no living thing dared harm her.

But no spirit appeared and that frightened her. Was she to die again after all her long troubles?

And then it happened and she knew a spirit had come to claim her. She saw nothing and heard nothing, only felt a warm presence, good and full of love. She knew what it was. It was the spirit of the great fruit tree among whose roots she had fallen into the pit.

And she heard in her mind a voice, as sweet as early morning birdsong, speaking to her. "She who was once

Dita, I claim you for my own and you are now a witch, with all a witch's powers."

And the new person's heart filled with joy. The voice went on. "I know you have deceived the priest, as you know you have, but you did not do it purposely. You have endured a great deal and you have been strong and brave. You have done all things properly and you are fit for the honor that has come to you. But you must remember always to use your powers wisely and for good. And never can you use them on yourself or to further your own aims. You cannot make yourself stronger or more comely or heal your wizened arm. If you do, then you will cease to be a witch and become Dita again."

The new person shuddered as though a cold wind had blown upon her. Some small part of her had known this all along, some small part of her had expected it. But she was not truly prepared for it, and it was as though on a summer day an icy wind had struck her. Nevertheless she said nothing and listened carefully.

"As long as you remember this," said the spirit of the fruit tree, "then you may be a witch and your name will be Halana and you will live in happiness and respect."

And then the presence was gone, but in Halana's hand was a branch of the great fruit tree, with leaves and blossoms and fruit.

She returned to the priest and told him all that the spirit had said to her, except the words about the deception. This, she knew, was something the spirit would want her to tell no one—and Halana herself had been a little surprised when she recognized that it was true. And now that she was Halana, it was no longer true, for Dita was dead and Halana was alive.

There was a celebration in the village to welcome the new witch. And many people brought Halana small gifts and told her they were glad to have a witch among them, for the priest needed help and no boy in the village had come forward to seek the training needed. Nor had any boy been singled out in any way to show that the spirits favored him and wished him for a priest.

So Halana took up her duties as a witch. At first she did small things. She helped find lost objects of little value and protected children against the stings of certain annoying insects.

But soon the priest called on her to do more important things, to help the gardens thrive and cause a spring which had become foul to yield fresh water once again.

She became a person of much importance in the village. Young women came to her for charms to make certain young men look on them with favor and old women came to her for potions to take the ache from their knees and hands. A man whose disposition was so bad that he shouted at his children and threw things at his beasts and made his wife weep asked for Halana's help and she was able to make him better-tempered. She was pleased to be of service.

The work was difficult and often took more strength than she had known she possessed. But Halana always did her best and she was given many things as pay so that it did not matter that she had no possessions of her own. She lived in a small house on the priest's land and was well supplied with food and even owned two mild little beasts that she could easily tend. And she mattered very much to many people.

And still Nogaro had not asked any of the young women of the village to be his wife. Halana watched him now and again as he passed her house and she wondered.

And after some time the priest took her with him when he cared for people who were ill and she aided in the cures. And when, once in a while, the remedies failed, as once in a while they must, with him she was able to comfort those who had been parted from a mother or father, husband or wife or child.

And it seemed to Halana a good and worthwhile thing to be a witch, worth the long years of having been Dita, worth the old husband's pinches and even the long terrible days in the pit, when it had seemed that she was unloved and unwanted. Even when the work was longer and harder than she would have thought it possible to bear, it seemed a good thing.

The priest was pleased with her and her fame grew and sometimes, as her father had fetched the witch from a far village to cure her mother, sometimes from far away men and women came to ask her help or guidance.

And then one day Nogaro's father came to her.

"I hope you keep well," he said.

"I am well," she answered. "And you and your family?"

Nogaro's father looked troubled.

"We are in good health," he said. "But I am concerned about my son Nogaro. He is long past the age to choose a wife and have a family of his own. He is a fine young man and a good hunter and any of the young women of the town would be pleased to marry him. I would like you to provide something that would cause him to look with love upon one of these young women, so that he would want to marry her. I myself would prefer that he marry Manika, daughter of Tadar, for she is a person of many admirable qualities, and healthy and good-looking as well. But I would rather he chose anyone at all than go longer without a wife. My other son has been married for some time and I would wish Nogaro to be as happy."

Halana looked at him gravely.

"It is a difficult task you have asked of me," she said. "I must have time to prepare myself. Come back in two days and I will tell you if it is a thing I can properly do."

Nogaro's father left and Halana sat for a long while. She remembered the day she had become a witch and the icy cold wind that had touched her when the spirit had given its warning. She remembered how she had shuddered.

She got up at last and went into the forest and walked until she came to the old husband's house, falling down now and filled once more with dust and spiders. How miserable Dita had been there! How she had longed to be the wife of some good man, of Nogaro!

She walked away again and came to the foot of the

great fruit tree. At the priest's order the hole among the roots had been filled in and marked with a sacred sign. This was the most holy of Halana's three holy places and no one might come here without her permission. She waited now to feel the presence of the tree spirit, but it did not come. And after a while she spoke a few words to invoke the spirit and still nothing happened.

Was there no way? Would the spirit of the tree not help her to be a witch and still become Nogaro's wife? If she used her powers to make Nogaro choose her to wed, then she would no longer be a witch, only Dita, frail and thin and with a withered arm. Nogaro would have married a woman not able to care properly for a garden and beasts and children, when he was away hunting.

Nogaro was a good young man. If he loved her truly, he would not care about such things perhaps. But perhaps he would know that she had lost her powers as a witch in order to make him love her. It would seem to him a wicked thing and he would not love her truly. And she would no longer matter to him or anyone else.

The priest would revile her. She would be of no use to him and he would know that she had acted wrongly and selfishly. All his kindness to her and his hard work in teaching her would have meant less to her than being Nogaro's wife.

Halana wept. She longed to have the spirit of the great fruit tree come and tell her what to do and how to do it, how to make Nogaro choose her and still be a witch, someone able to be of service to her town, someone deserving of admiration and respect. But the spirit did not come.

And when darkness descended, Halana lay down upon the earth and wept still more, for she felt the icy wind and knew there was no help for her. And she implored the spirit to come and comfort her, but there was no response.

After two days she went back to the village. She went slowly, for the pain in her heart was great and seemed to make her limbs heavy and weary. When she returned to her house, Nogaro's father was waiting for her. He came to meet her and looked at her anxiously.

"Have I asked so much of you?" he asked. "You seem ill. Is this such a difficult task?"

"I am not ill," answered Halana. "The task you set me is not too difficult. I will do as you have requested. It will take a few days."

Nogaro's father was pleased. But Halana did not have to use her powers on Nogaro. The next day he went to Tadar and asked permission to marry his daughter Manika.

Halana went to the marriage and she wished them well, for they were strong and handsome and good and suited each other nicely. She hoped that all they did would thrive and prosper.

And Halana herself went about the affairs of her craft quietly and earnestly. She cured those who were ill and comforted children who had bad dreams and caused gardens to grow well.

And after some time she knew that the spirit of the great fruit tree, by its very silence, had given her wise advice.

She cured a man who suffered from terrible head-aches and helped a woman locate her favorite needle, which had been lost, and called forth warm weather in a lazy spring.

And after some time she knew that Dita was truly gone, that she was truly Halana, and she was happy again.

BY MARY Q. STEELE

Because of the Sand Witches There
The First of the Penguins
Journey Outside
The Owl's Kiss: Three Stories
The True Men
The Living Year (for adults)

AS WILSON GAGE

Big Blue Island
Dan and the Miranda
Down in the Boondocks
Ghost of Five Owl Farm
Mike's Toads
Miss Osborne-the-Mop
Squash Pie
A Wild Goose Tale

MARY Q. STEELE has written many popular books for children. Under the pen name of Wilson Gage she is the author of *Squash Pie* and *Down in the Boondocks,* both ALA Notable Books. Under her own name she is the author of *Journey Outside,* a Newbery Honor Book, as well as many other books, including *The True Men, The First of the Penguins,* and *Because of the Sand Witches There.*

Mary Q. Steele was born and raised in Tennessee. Today she lives in Signal Mountain, Tennessee, with her husband William O. Steele, who is also a writer.